Run, Killer, Run

run, killer, run

William Campbell Gault

Adams Media

New York   London   Toronto   Sydney   New Delhi

Adams Media
An Imprint of Simon & Schuster, Inc.
57 Littlefield Street
Avon, Massachusetts 02322

For information about special discounts for bulk purchases, please contact Simon & Schuster Special Sales at 1-866-506-1949 or business@simonandschuster.com.

Manufactured in the United States of America

10 9 8 7 6 5 4 3 2 1

Library of Congress Cataloging-in-Publication Data has been applied for.

ISBN 978-1-4405-5795-8
ISBN 978-1-4405-3916-9 (ebook)

This work has been previously published in print format by:
The Crowell-Collier Publishing Company.

For ELLA HOVDE GAULT
My ma

Run, Killer, Run

Chapter 1

AT THE door of the cheap motel room, he paused for a moment, his hand on the knob. Then he pushed out into the biting sunlight of the uncovered porch. He walked along that to the office and went through the sagging screen door.

Post cards and curios and the smell of coffee. A fat man sat in a big rattan rocker near the stove, reading a Phoenix paper. He looked up blandly.

"Sleep all right?"

"Fine," he lied. "When is check-out time?"

"Well—we ain't too fussy. We usually figure around four o'clock. That good enough?"

He nodded and turned toward the door.

The fat man asked, "Heading west?"

There was probably nothing in the voice but his imagination. But he felt the moment's tension and turned slowly. He kept his voice casual. "Yes. Why?"

The man yawned. "Just wondered. Everybody's going west, it seems. No work out there, though. Everybody and his brother in California, now. Don't ask me why."

"My mother lives there," he lied. "Where's the best place to eat in town?"

"There isn't any you'd call 'best.' I guess *Sam's Barbecue* is the least worst. Don't order no fried potatoes, though; they'll kill you. Do me, at least."

"That's right on the main street?"

"Yup."

"Thanks," he said and went out into the glare, again. This was the first time he'd risked an appearance in the bright light of day; he walked with a feigned limp, keeping his face turned toward the store fronts, as though looking for someone he knew.

Why the limp? he suddenly asked himself. It was something that had occurred to him without reason, and he tried to analyze it. Was it a kind of self-pity, a physical request for pity from the society from which he was outlawed? He'd seen too much of that self-pity behind the walls; he stopped limping.

Sam's Barbecue boasted a huge neon sign, high on the flat-roofed building. And a sign in the window proclaimed "*Air Conditioned.*" Strangely enough, it was true.

He sat at the counter, avoiding the direct gaze of any of the other patrons. The waitress was a short and shapely straw blonde. She set a glass of water within reach and waited, looking past him.

"Ribs," he said, "with a baked potato. Green salad."

"Want a cup of coffee while you're waiting?"

"If you please."

She glanced at him briefly and turned to get him the coffee. She set it in front of him and walked toward the kitchen.

The sugar bowl was two stools farther up the counter. He stretched, reaching for it. In this position, his face came opposite the mirrored section of the back bar and he saw the girl in the booth.

His hand paused, trembled. He knew he had seen her some place before. He was sure they'd been introduced. Her eyes met his briefly in the mirror and quickly looked away. His hand was still trembling as he brought the sugar dispenser toward him.

Dark, short hair and intelligent, level blue eyes. A slim, tanned girl. *Where, where, where. . . ?*

His mouth was dry. He finished the water and put the ice from the tumbler into his steaming coffee. The juke box started up in a wailing hillbilly lament, drowning out the voice of the girl behind him. She was now ordering.

The place was too cool, but sweat ran down the back of his hands and dribbled onto the Formica counter top. He closed his eyes for a second and saw the walls and the bars. It served him right, walking into a place as public as this, right on the main highway through town. And at noon. How damnably, damnably stupid. If she knew him, she knew his history. If she remembered him, she might have told the waitress something when he thought she was ordering. . . .

He watched the waitress as she came around the bend in the counter. The phone was there, next to the cash register.

But she walked past it. Nor did she look his way.

He stared at his coffee cup until she brought his order. "Something wrong, mister?"

He looked up quickly and shook his head. "Why?"

"You look sick."

He took a deep breath. "Too much sun, I guess. And I'm hungrier than I should be. Would you bring more coffee, please?"

He forced himself to eat leisurely, never showing the girl in the booth his profile, keeping an eye on the waitress to see if she might be transferring a message.

Where had he seen that girl? Who was she? There'd been no recognition in her brief glance, but he was sure he'd met her.

A casual acquaintance who hadn't read about him in the papers? Somebody's wife? A secretary? Theatrical? No, no, no. . . .

Behind him, the door opened, closed with a hiss of the pneumatic silencer. Warm air washed past him and was absorbed by the cooling system.

A pair of uniformed men took the two stools to his right. The waitress was moving toward them and there seemed to be some anticipation in her gaze.

They were state troopers.

He stilled the impulse to flee, staring at his coffee cup. And then his eyes lifted to the waitress searching her face as she approached the pair of officers. She was smiling.

One of them said, "My girl, my little Velma. What's good today, honey?"

"Everything's good at Sam's, " she told him. "You mean 'what's cheap,' don't you, Ernie?"

The officer's partner laughed. "You got Ernie pegged, kid." He looked down the counter. "How about those ribs?"

"A dollar, ten. What else do you want to know?"

They laughed.

He slid a quarter under his plate and asked, "Could I have a check, please?"

"Sure, mister. You all right, now?" She was leafing through her book.

Both of the troopers looked at him; he could almost feel their scrutiny. He said quietly, "I'm all right." He took the

11

slip she extended to him.

For a moment, it seemed, his legs weren't going to work. He put a hand on the counter to steady himself. Now, all three of them were staring at him and nausea swirled in him.

"Just a second, Mac," one of the troopers said. "You look sick."

"No," he said hoarsely. "I'm all right. I'm fine. The air is all I—" Desperately, he moved away from the counter.

And bumped into the girl who'd risen from the booth. Her meal was almost untouched.

She looked up at him and he caught the quick warning in her eyes. She said humbly, "I'm sorry. It was all my fault. You were right. I'll come home. We'll go home together."

One of the troopers was grinning, now. The girl looked directly at him and smiled. "He's been worrying about me. He isn't going to have to worry any more." She put a bill on the counter and then came back to his side.

As they went out, he heard the waitress say, "Love, see Ernie? *That's* love."

Laughter.

Outside, he looked at the check, still in his hand. The girl took it from him and went back inside.

Now, he thought. Now would be the time to run. Whatever her pitch is, this would be the best time to get out of here. But if he ran, those troopers would see him. And where could a man run to, in this town? This was no huge city with a million doorways. There was simply no place to hide. He waited.

She came out again, and said softly, "My car's right up here near the corner."

He fell in step beside her. "You know me?"

"Tom Spears," she said. "Am I right?"

He didn't answer.

"I'm a friend," she went on. "You don't remember me?"

He didn't look at her. "No."

She stopped to open the door of a black *Plymouth* convertible at the curb. It was the car that had left the motel court, just before noon. It was carrying California plates.

He said, "You were trying to find me? Didn't you inquire

at that motel this morning?"

"Yes. Though not under your true name. I was Joe Hubbard's fiancée. Now, do you remember?"

Joe Hubbard had been his attorney. Joe had fought a desperate, bitter, loosing fight to save his friend's neck.

He looked at the girl, and now he remembered. Joe's office, a long time ago. He looked at the open car door and said, "Don't tell me Joe sent you? Is he crazy?"

"He's dead," she said. "He was murdered." Her voice was rough. "Don't you read the papers?" Her dark eyes were suddenly wet.

He felt the nausea whirl in him again, and the sun seemed unbearable. "Murdered—? Joe Hubbard murd—?"

She pushed him roughly. "Get in the car. Don't stand there, yammering like an idiot for heaven's sake."

He got in and sat stiffly in the seat. Joe Hubbard, the oversized Galahad. Genial Joe Hubbard, the man who'd come so gallantly to the defense of Tom Spears, the bookie with the millionaire wife.

It didn't add. It didn't figure. He'd known Joe in L.A., played golf with him, gone sailing with him. But he'd never dared hope that Joe, with his ethics, would come all the way to St. Louis to handle the murder trial defense of Tom Spears.

The girl was behind the wheel now and her perfume was faint on the hot, dry air. "We'll go back and get what you have at that motel. We'll drive straight through."

"Why were you looking for me? If you were? Did you come here, to this town, looking for me?"

"That's right. I went as far east as Prescott. I knew the desert would be your big obstacle. I'd better not drive into that court; the proprietor will remember I was asking for a Ned Allis, and if he sees us, together——" She took a breath.

"How did you know I was using the name Ned Allis?"

"I learned it from a man in St. Louis, a man named Chuck. I phoned him."

He shook his head wearily, and leaned back a bit. "Do you realize what you're doing? I'm a fugitive from justice."

"I don't think you are. I think you're a fugitive from the law, but not from justice."

"That's quibbling. Does that matter?"

"It does to me," she said quietly. "Would you rather go it alone?"

He closed his eyes, thinking back on the lonely, frightened trail up to this moment. He said, "I insist on it."

"Why?"

"I won't have anyone innocent involved."

"You're innocent, aren't you?"

"Of murder, yes. But not of running away. That's a crime, too, you know."

"And I'm already implicated in that," she pointed out. "Those officers back at the restaurant will remember me. And, being implicated, I've a stake now in seeing that you don't get caught here in Arizona." She had stopped the car and pulled to the side of the road. "Go get your extra shirt or whatever you were carrying. I'll wait here."

He looked at her and then over at the motel to his left. He got out of the car and walked along in the shade of the long building to his room.

There was only his jacket and his razor and an extra shirt. He stood quietly a moment in the bleak, hot room. It was a bad decision to make. She seemed like a nice girl and if she was caught with him she would be implicated. But, as she had said, she was already implicated in Arizona.

He turned and went out.

As he got into the car, she said, "I wasn't sure you'd be back. I thought you might have conditioned yourself to running away."

He said nothing.

She put the car into gear, her eyes on the road ahead. She went through the gears to high and settled for an even fifty miles an hour. This was foothill country; they'd climb into the mountains and through them before the real desert started.

She said, "I think Route 89 to Wickenburg would be best and then 60 to Blythe. That's the shorter way, I believe."

He watched the road unwind. "I guess." Then: "Why are you helping me?"

A pause before she answered. "I don't honestly know. Except that nobody else seemed to be volunteering. And I thought that maybe—well, what happened to you might be tied up with Joe."

The car was climbing and he felt the pressure building up inside his ears. He closed his eyes and leaned back deeper into the cushions. For the first time in four days, lassitude came to his taut body. The hum of the motor was remote in his consciousness, growing dimmer, fading into nothing. He slept.

He wakened to a world of sand and sage. Directly ahead, the rim of the sun was visible above the horizon. She had pulled the visor down and was squinting at the shimmering black road, her lovely face slack in fatigue.

He said, "I'd better drive for a while. You look tired. How long did I sleep?"

"I don't know." She was slowing the car. "We stopped for gas and you slept right through it. Are you hungry?"

"Starved. God knows what kind of eating places we'll find out here, though."

The car had stopped now, at the side of the road. "There's a place that's been advertised a lot—*The Last Resort*. It would have to be better than it sounds." She got out and stood at the side of the car, stretching, arching her back, moving her head from side to side.

Tom slid over. When she got in, again, he said, "I shouldn't have slept. It must have been a grind."

"That's all right, though I could have used some talk. It's not good to be quiet too long, is it?"

He went through the gears before answering. "Quiet too long—? I don't understand."

"A person broods. You must have, in that place. Would it do any good to talk—to talk about St. Louis?"

He kept his eyes on the road. "There's nothing to talk about. That was her home, originally; she maintained a house there. She went for a quick trip, one of her whims, after a quarrel we'd had." He paused, to adjust the visor to the lower sun.

"And you followed her?"

Tom nodded. "On the next plane. When I walked into the house, she was dead." He paused again. "But nobody ever be-

15

lieved that, including the jury."

The girl was silent a moment. Then, "You said she *maintained* a house in St. Louis. That would mean servants if she kept it ready for occupancy."

"There was only a housekeeper at this place while she was away. The housekeeper wasn't there when I walked in. She later claimed she'd been given the day off."

"Why?"

Tom glanced at the girl and back at the road. "Why—? How would I know why?"

Her voice was almost a whisper. "You poor damned fool, can't you guess? You know your wife was a tramp, don't you. Everybody else knew, but I suppose—"

His brain seemed to erupt and the road ahead wavered. He said harshly, "You're insane. What kind of—" The car slowed as he stared at her.

"Look out!" she said, and he turned to pull the car back onto the road in time.

"We'll talk about it later," she said quietly. "I was rude and stupid. We'll talk about it later."

Ahead, and all around them the limitless desert stretched, dotted with sage and cacti. He wanted to stop, to leave the car, to send her on her way. Why didn't he? Did he half believe her? He drove on steadily.

It was dusk, now. To his right, a sign read: *The Last Resort—One Mile. Best Steaks West of Chicago. If You Can't Stop, Wave When You Go By.*

It was almost dark and the next minute it was. He fumbled for the light switch, found it, switched on the high beam with his foot.

"I'm truly sorry," she said. "It was rotten, throwing those remarks at you."

He kept his voice even. "It's something I had to take. I'm a long way from home. And without friends."

The Last Resort was a typical tourist trap of logs, with wagon wheels flanking the entrance.

The girl said, "If you want, I can get some sandwiches and coffee. If you'd rather stay out here."

He glanced at the parking lot. "There aren't any cars around. It will probably be all right to go in." He studied her

16

in the glow from the instrument panel. "I don't even know your name."

"It's Jean. Jean Revolt. I thought you might have remembered."

He nodded. "I remember now." He took a deep breath. "You might think me ungrateful. Lord knows you had enough trouble of your own, and then coming to find me——" He shook his head. "I've been running so long, I'm not exactly human, any more."

She asked, "Is that all you're going to do——*run?*"

He smiled bitterly. "That's what I should have done, right from the start, right from the second I found her dead in St. Louis. Yes, that's all I'm going to do——*run.*"

Her voice was anxious. "Then why to Los Angeles? I thought you were coming back to *fight.*"

"What's there to fight? The law? I'm going to get some money in Los Angeles and then head for Mexico. Who would I fight?"

"Whoever framed you. Whoever sent Joe to St. Louis to put on the weakest, most professionally shameful defense of his career."

He stared at her. "Joe? Joe fought like a badger. He wore himself out."

She shook her head slowly. "Don't tell me that. I studied law. He picked the worst jury he could collect and hammered away at the weakest arguments to offer them. Any criminal lawyer will tell you what a butchery he made of the case."

Tom expelled his breath. After a few moments, he said, "When you told me about him, about his being murdered—— When you talked about that, this noon, there were tears in your eyes. And now you tell me this."

"I loved him," Jean said. "Even though I saw he could be bought, I loved him. But loving him didn't cut off my reasoning powers."

He turned off the car lights and opened the door on his side. "I don't know what to believe, any more. Joe Hubbard ——why, hell, we used to kid him about being the modern Galahad. I'm no lily, you know, and the men I worked with are in a hazardous trade. But Joe——"

"I've talked enough about that," she said, and got out.

17

They walked together up to the porch running the length of the building and he held the door open for her.

The lights were dim. There were steer heads on the walls and Indian blankets and copies of Remington drawings. The ceilings were beamed; the floor pegged planking. TLR was branded into the tables and chairs.

There were two waitresses standing near the cash register. In charge of the cash register was a stocky, dark woman.

"Evenin', folks," she called, as though Chicago were forgotten. "Set right down to the best meal you've et on the road."

They took a table in one of the dimmer corners, and Tom held Jean's chair for her.

"You don't seem like a bookie, at all," she said. "You——"

"I'm not, any more," he interrupted. "Know many bookies?"

She smiled. "None, until that day in Joe's office."

The waitress brought their menus and Tom asked Jean, "Would you like a drink before dinner?"

Her smile was wan. "Whiskey and water. Bourbon."

"A pair," he told the waitress. "We'll order after that."

The waitress went away. From behind the register, the short, dark woman called, "Come far today, folks?"

"From Newark, New Jersey," Tom told her. "We made good time until we hit the mountains."

The woman frowned and glanced wonderingly at the waitress.

Jean said softly, "It was a poor joke, but a joke. I'm surprised you can make any kind of joke."

"I surprised myself," Tom admitted. "Maybe Mexico looks closer, or maybe you've given me some hope. You're a fighter, all right, aren't you?"

She nodded. "I had to fight in my neighborhood. They're after a girl, there, from the time she's twelve."

"And you've undoubtedly *always* been a beautiful girl."

"Well, thank you, Mr. Spears." She made a face. "You're coming back to normal."

Behind them, the door slammed. Jean was facing the door and Tom didn't turn to see who'd entered. He kept his gaze on her face, awaiting a reaction.

"Tourists," she said.

From behind the register, the woman called, "Howdy, folks. If you got the money, we got the grub."

Jean said. "The Texas Guinan of Route 60. Maybe she doesn't expect repeat business."

A short, fat man and a tall, thin woman walked past them and chose a table nearby. A girl of about twelve trailed them.

They were a harmless enough trio but Tom found himself watching them. Then Jean made a face and shook her head. He nodded.

They finished their drinks and ordered steaks. Over their coffee, Tom said, "I'll drive the rest of the way, if you want. Try to get some rest."

"I'll try. I'm—bushed."

The night air was clear and cold; the stars seemed to be just out of reach. They were about ten miles from the state line; they would cross the Colorado at Blythe.

As they crossed the parking lot to the car, he noticed how slowly and tiredly Jean moved. It must have been some hunt for her, this trip.

He held the door open for her and went around to climb behind the wheel. The car would be inspected at Blythe; he'd have to get out and unlock the luggage compartment under the lights of the station.

Well, they weren't cops. . . .

The motor hummed in the quiet night. Next to him in the seat, Jean's head was back and her eyes partially closed. Headlights showed miles up the road, wavering like illuminated butterflies.

He thought of Joe Hubbard and what Jean had told him about Joe. There'd be no reason for her to lie. And if there were these defects in Joe, who could be flawless? In his business, a certain amount of faith was necessary. It was a growing business and attracting all sorts of trash, but the men Tom had dealt with played the cold percentage, scorning the angles.

Granted they were outside the law, they answered what seemed to be a universal desire, the urge to gamble. And it was a strange law that set the state up in a business considered otherwise illegal and socially undesirable.

In that seamy world, he had done business and prospered. Joe Hubbard had been one friend outside that world. So had

19

Lois, Tom's wife. Both of them outside his workaday world and high above it in the social scale.

Yet, Joe. . . ? Tom shook his head. Maybe Joe, but nobody could poison his memory of Lois.

The girl in the seat was sleeping now, her face softer in repose, lovelier. Why had she been so vehement about Lois?

The Colorado was beneath them, now; ahead were the lights of Blythe. Like a mirage it was, from the desert to the unexpected greenness of Blythe, and then back to the gray desert, once they would leave the town. Like a theatrical city, set up by the Chamber of Commerce.

The lights of the checking station were brilliant; the attendants were uniformed. Tom's capacity for fright was dulled, but there was a dryness in his mouth and his breathing was work.

The attendant smiled. "Local car. Won't take a minute, sir. It's these Florida crackers we worry about."

Tom said evenly, "No fruit, no bugs. Nothing but a sleeping beauty." He forced himself to face the man squarely.

When he got back into the car, Jean was still sleeping and he started gently, accelerating gradually.

She slept and he drove. He thought of Lois, the three years of their marriage, fine, full years.

He remembered her saying, one time, "If I should ever feel a serious urge for infidelity, I won't embarrass you, dear. I'll get out of town, where you won't know about it."

She had a penchant for meaningless words and he hadn't given this statement of hers any serious consideration.

"That," she had continued, "is what my faithless female friends tell me *they* do. So if I should ever take a trip—"

Tom closed his eyes for a moment as a chill moved through him.

As they came into Indio, Jean stirred and sat erectly. "Welcome home," she said. "No trouble?"

"None."

She yawned and peered at the instrument board. "You were about to have some. We need gas. What have you been thinking of?"

"My wife."

Nothing from Jean.

He pulled into an all-night station and told the attendant, "Fill her up. And you'd better check the oil."

Jean stared bleakly through the windshield at nothing.

Tom said, "It hurt—when you called her a tramp. I realize, now, that you wouldn't be fly-brained enough to say a thing like that unless you had reason to."

She didn't look at him. "Thank you."

He watched the attendant lift the hood, his mind back in St. Louis, remembering that first shocking glimpse of Lois' dead face and open, staring eyes.

Jean asked, "Have you a cigarette?"

He gave her one and held a light for her. Her eyes were dull, her face slightly puffed from sleep.

The attendant came around to his side of the car. "Oil's okay, sir. That'll be four-twenty."

Jean fumbled for her purse, but Tom paid it, and said, "If you want to tell me about—about Lois, more about her, I'd—" He was pulling out onto the highway again.

Her voice was dull. "There's nothing to tell, really. A girl gets a remark here and there from reliable sources and I suppose I reasoned that where there was smoke there had to be fire. Anyway, it could have been all lies and what's to be gained by discussing it now?"

"Probably nothing. But for a girl who stuck her neck way, way out, chasing around the country after me, you must have had a change of mind."

She nodded. "I've been thinking about you." She opened the window on her side and threw her cigarette out. "I've been remembering what a patsy you were. And now you tell me you're going to run to Mexico. That doesn't coincide with my picture of the man I thought I'd be helping."

He said quietly, "I changed my mind about Mexico. While you were sleeping."

Her voice came to life. "Tom—! That's wonderful, Tom. We'll work out something—"

He turned to see her beaming at him. "*We* won't do anything. I'll do what I can, but I won't have you involved any further."

"All right." She paused to chuckle. "All right, *master*. But where are you going in Los Angeles? Is there someone you can trust?"

"There's one man, at least. I hope he's home. Whatever happens, though, Jean, I'm not going back. I'm never going back to jail."

She didn't answer. He kept his eyes on the black road, unwinding under the probe of the headlights, his thoughts back at that place of bars and stone walls and defeated men. By the time he got to Riverside, she was sleeping again.

In Culver City, he pulled to the curb about a block from his destination. Her eyes flickered open and then she sat erectly in the seat.

"There's a lot I'd like to say," he told her quietly, "but I'm no Shakespeare. What you've done for me isn't anything I'll ever forget. If things break right, I'll look you up."

"Look me up either way, Tom." She paused. "This friend you're going to now—is he a gambler?"

He nodded.

"Well, won't they be watching those kind of friends? I mean the police would naturally have them under observation."

"I'll be careful. Gamblers are the only friends I have, Jean. Except for you. And if the police should bother you, admit nothing. They'll never implicate you from my end."

She put a tentative hand on his shoulder. "Be very careful, won't you? And phone me?"

He opened the door and got out. "I'll be careful. And you be careful. And thank you, again." His hand trembled as he closed the door, and waved. Then he turned, and walked off.

He heard the Plymouth move away and he didn't turn around. The tension was back, the desire to run, to seek the shadows.

Chapter 2

THE HAVEN he was approaching through the dark night was a triplex of dark gray stucco, and Jud had the rear unit. Tom moved quietly along the walk, listening, watching; all the fears he had left in Arizona had again come to life.

He pressed the button and heard the single chime from within. It was a lot to ask a friend, to harbor a fugitive from justice, an escaped convict who'd been jailed for murder.

He heard footsteps and then Jud's careful voice. "Who's there?" The light overhead didn't go on.

"It's Tom Spears, Jud."

The door opened quickly and quietly and the tall, thin body of Jud Shallock was framed in the doorway. He was wearing pajama bottoms and nothing else. "Come in, boy. Quick. Don't stand in the light."

Tom stepped into the dim living room and Jud quickly closed the door. Then the lanky man turned to put a hand on Tom's shoulder. "I've been worried about you. How the hell did you make it?"

"I'm here. How're things going with the boys?"

"Things are very rocky. The heat's on. I hope to hell nobody was watching this place." He went around the room, closing the Venetian blinds. Then he flopped into a big chair near the entrance to the kitchen, and regarded Tom gravely.

Tom was sitting on the davenport, leaning forward, the tension still with him. "Is the heat temporary or permanent? Just for the newspapers, maybe?"

Jud shrugged wearily. "Who knows? It catches the small fry, anyway." His voice showed more emotion. "The small fry—that's us, Tom."

"Not me," Tom said. "Not any more. No cop would consider me small fry. Nannie in town?"

Nannie Koronas was Mr. Big to them, though they didn't deal with him directly. Nannie was the boss, they knew, though they would have a hard time proving it in court.

Jud nodded. "He bought a new house. In Westwood. Going to hit him for getaway money, Tom?"

Tom shook his head. "Not yet." A pause. "Heard anything around, Jud?"

The tall man frowned. "Like what—?"

"Like who killed Lois."

Jud stared at him for seconds, saying nothing.

Tom said, "My God, you don't think I—?"

23

"I didn't think anything, Tom. I didn't think about it either way, or mean to judge you. I figured you *might* have caught her with—" He broke off, coloring.

Tom stared at him, his heart hammering. "With *who*, Jud?"

Jud's face was tight. "How do I know with who? With any good-looking, fast talking—Oh, what the hell difference does it make, now?"

Tom said nothing. He was breathing heavily and there was a faintness in his chest.

Jud said, "I'm sorry. I thought you knew. The boys figured you might have bumped her, but that you had reason and— Tom, if you feel like hitting me, go ahead. I thought you knew."

Tom asked, "Hearsay, Jud? Or do you know she was unfaithful?"

Jud shrugged. "I never peeped, if that's what you mean. I'd make book on it, though. Let's get off the subject, Tom."

"Why? Maybe, if I knew who her last lover had been, I'd learn what happened in St. Louis."

Jud's face was blank and his voice dry. "I don't know anything about that. I don't like to talk about the dead, Tom."

Tom studied him for seconds, first in anger and then in resignation. Jud could be the stubbornest man alive when he wanted to. Tom asked, "Do you want to talk about Joe Hubbard?"

"I don't know anything about that, either. Do you want to talk about him?"

"I was wondering if he was one of Lois' boy friends."

"Not to my knowledge. He was your friend, Tom. The rest of the boys didn't know him. He wasn't in our world." Jud put his legs over the arm of the chair, his bare feet dangling. "What made you think his death was connected to your wife's?"

"He defended me."

Jud smiled. "And how. A bull-pen lawyer would have done a better job. Some friend he was, Tom."

Tom said nothing, staring at the rug.

Jud stood up. "You must be bushed. You take the bed; I'll sleep out here on the davenport."

Tom started to protest, but Jud waved a hand. "I want you in the bedroom. I'm harboring a fugitive and I want you as well hidden as I can get you. That much, I demand."

Tom rose wearily. "All right. You're the boss. To-night."

In the bedroom, Tom pulled off his shoes and trousers and socks and flopped into bed in his underwear. There was a pain behind his eyes and at the roots of his upper molars. Sinusitis?

He stretched on his back, staring at the dark ceiling. It seemed that everybody knew about Lois. . . .He'd thought she was special, a long trip up the social ladder from him, an aristocrat. His beautiful, witty, social register Lois, how he had loved her.

And loved her still.

He slept without dreams and wakened to a hot, bright room. Through the closed door, he could hear Jud talking on the phone. He rose and took his razor with him into the bathroom.

Jud was in the kitchen when Tom finished dressing. Jud asked, "How do you like your eggs?"

"Sunnyside up." Tom sat down at the small, square table in an ell of the kitchen.

Jud took a quartet of eggs from the refrigerator. "I tried to get Nannie. Somebody at the house said he wasn't in town."

Tom smiled. "You're supposed to go through channels to Nannie Koronas, Jud. Privates don't speak directly to generals. Why did you want to talk to him?"

"You'll need money, won't you? You don't expect to hang around this town, do you?"

"I'll need money. But I'm not leaving town right away. I'm through running, Jud. For a while, anyway."

Jud paused in the act of cracking an egg. "What can you do but run? This town's too hot for you, Tom."

"Maybe. But maybe there's a line here to what happened to Lois. If there is, I want to get onto it. Nannie should know a few things. He's got friends in St. Louis and Chicago and every place else where people gamble."

Jud shook his head. "Nannie knows the gamblers. Was Lois killed by a gambler?"

"Who knows?" Tom said dully. "But after Lois, Joe Hubbard was killed. He was killed in this town and Nannie could very well have the word on that. He has a lot of ears in this town."

Jud nodded. "Yeah, that's true enough." He brought over a pair of eggs for Tom, and pushed a basket of breakfast rolls closer. "Nannie could know, but he's no stoolie. Why don't you forget both of them, Tom?"

Tom stared at him. "Aren't you forgetting I've been convicted of murder? I want to be a free man."

"In Mexico, you'd be free. This town is full of cops and they'll be looking for you. Nannie probably has connections in Mexico; you could change your name and live like a king on American money down there."

Tom shook his head.

Jud went over to get his own eggs. He sat down across from Tom. "In our business, we play the percentage. The smart way is to get out, Tom, get out while you can."

"I'm not running. Let's not talk about that."

They were silent for minutes. Tom thought of Jud's words and appreciated the wisdom of them. The law was all around them and the big boys were on top. Jean had sold him a different bill of goods last night, but this was a bright morning and a time to face reality. He was no Hawkshaw, no crusader, no superman. He was just one of the small men in a big business, quietly making a living on the percentage.

They were finishing their coffee when the door chime sounded.

Jud said, "In the bathroom. In the shower stall. Quick!"

Tom was in the shower stall, the opaque glass door closed, when Jud opened the front door.

The bathroom door was open and he could hear Jud say, "Sergeant Kurtz—what an unpleasant surprise this is."

Tom knew him and the sergeant knew them all. He was a county man and gambling was his detail.

The sergeant's voice was mild. "Morning, Jud. Aren't you going to invite me in?"

"I was just going out, Sergeant. Something on your mind?"

"Yup. Tom Spears. Seen him?"

"Tom Spears? Is he in town? Did you get word *he* was in town, Sergeant?"

26

"Cut out the ham. I'm not stupid, you know. What's wrong with my coming in?"

"Nothing except the lack of a warrant in your hand. Did you come here to look for Tom? We're not exactly buddies, you know."

"Save the dramatics, Shallock. If you haven't anything to hide, there shouldn't be anything to prevent my coming in."

"Nothing but the Constitution," Jud said, and his voice was ice. "Nothing except that this is my home and I don't like cops."

"I see." A long silence. "Okay, Shallock, we'll play it that way. I've given you more than one break in the past. But covering a murder would put you into a different file. I think you'd better come along with me."

"On what charge?"

"I'll think of one on the way. Let's go. Are you resisting arrest?"

Another long silence and then the slam of the door.

In the shower stall, Tom felt the sweat drip off his wrists, trickle down his sides. He was sure the beat of his heart could be heard in the living room.

Had the sergeant come in or had Jud gone out? He'd heard nothing beyond the slam of the door. Then, from outside, he heard the grind of a starter, and he expelled the breath he'd been holding.

Slowly, he opened the shower door and stepped over the high sill. He peered around the edge of the bathroom door and saw the empty living room. He started to breathe steadily and the pounding of his heart diminished.

The sudden jangle of the phone stopped him as he was heading toward the kitchen. He stared at it. A trick? No, there hadn't been time, yet, for Sergeant Kurtz to try a trick.

And it could be a friend. It could even be Nannie.

He lifted the phone from its cradle and said guardedly, "Hello."

It was Jean's voice. "Tom——? This is you, isn't it? Tom——?"

He asked, "Who is it, please?"

"Jean Revolt. Tom, are you all right? I thought you'd head for that place. I knew he was your friend. Are you all right? *Answer me.*"

"Jud was just picked up by a man from the Sheriff's Department. I'm still here. But they'll be back. I'm running, again, Jean. You were wrong. I wouldn't have a chance. I'm running."

"How? On foot? You fool! I'll pick you up. If you want to run, that's your business, but let me give you a good start."

"No. I don't want you implicated. I'm leaving right now. I won't be here by the time you get here. Good-bye, Jean."

"Wait—!" Her voice was shrill, hurting his ear. "If you leave, I'll tell them I helped you come from Arizona. I will, Tom. If you run, now, I did wrong in helping you and I'll tell the police. I'll be implicated, then, right up to my ears. That's a promise, Tom."

Annoyance moved through him, but he knew she would do as she threatened. He said, "It's my life, Jean."

"And believing in your innocence was a part of my life. But if you run, now, what I did was wrong, too. And I'm going to right it by going to the police. Tom, I've had legal training. Believe in me. I'm more concerned with justice than the letter of the law."

"You've never spent time behind those bars. You don't know what you're saying."

Her voice was low. "I can't argue over a phone. Where can I pick you up?"

He paused, and then said, "There's a bar on Braddock and Mentone, in Culver City. Could you find that?"

"I could, and will."

"I'll be waiting there."

"You promise?"

"I promise."

After he'd hung up, he checked the bedroom to see if he had left any match books or any other signs of his presence. Then he went out the back door and into the fenced yard.

There was an alley, here, and another alley bisecting it a hundred feet beyond. He took the second alley, walking carefully, watching for any sign of the law.

If the sergeant had really believed Jud was hiding him, the neighborhood would be alive with cops, right now. But there were none in sight as he left the alley behind and turned onto a quiet residential street fronted with small homes.

28

Two blocks away, he knew, was the business district and he'd have to go through that to get to the bar. Culver City had its own police force and it was a well patrolled town.

He saw no squad car as he approached the business district. But the urge to hurry, to keep to the shadows was strong in him. He resisted it, walking leisurely past the super market, the filling stations. As he crossed the main street, all the sunlight in the area seemed to be focused on him.

He was in a pedestrian lane, and the traffic had to stop. In the lane nearest the other side of the street, a squad car slowed and waited.

Tom kept his eyes straight ahead, quickening his pace a trifle, as any Milquetoast citizen would who was holding up the law. He reached the curb without being accosted, and slowed his pace again.

Each step away from the corner seemed to take a full minute. He was halfway into the block before his breathing went back to normal.

Herbie's Hubby Haven was a red brick building next to a small parking lot. There were no cars in the parking lot this morning, though there was an ancient Chev parked in front. Tom went up the two steps that led to the narrow door.

He'd been here only once before, with Jud, and there was little chance that the bartender would remember him. He was in luck; the man behind the bar wasn't the same one who'd been here the other time.

Tom ordered a bottle of eastern beer and sat at a table near the huge front window where he could see the street.

The bartender said, "How about them Braves moving to Milwaukee, huh? Think it'll go through?"

"Hard to tell," Tom said. He hadn't even read about it.

"If you ask me, I think it's stupid," the man went on.

Who asked you? Tom thought. He said, "Maybe."

"What's wrong with L.A.?" the man persisted. "Here's a town of two million crying for major league ball. Milwaukee, huh!"

Tom smiled.

"You new out here?" the man asked.

Tom shook his head. "Why?"

"You're kind of pale. Work inside, I suppose, huh?"

Tom nodded.

"Well, it beats me. It ain't right."

"Maybe we can get the Browns," Tom said. "They're losing money in St. Louis."

"Baltimore couldn't get 'em. You work at Douglas?"

Tom shook his head. "I used to work for *Mayfair*, but I've had an operation. I've been off for two weeks."

"Oh. I thought you looked kind of peaked. You been in here before, much?"

Tom shook his head. "I don't drink much. Just a bottle of beer at home once in a while."

The man nodded. "You're smart. Like I tell my wife, I just wish I had the money some of these working stiffs spend over a bar. I'd drive a Cad. And they ain't got change for a nickel the day before payday. The next depression, won't they be sorry they didn't salt a few bucks? Aw, people give me a pain in the ass."

Tom smiled. "You're in the wrong business if you don't like people."

"I know. But I liked 'em before I got into this business, before I saw this side of 'em." He lighted a cigarette. "How do they pay at *Mayfair*, if it ain't too personal?"

"Good," Tom said. "We're pretty well organized."

"How good?"

Tom shrugged, trying to think of a figure. "Oh, I take home around seventy bucks each week."

"Seventy take-home? How many kids?"

"One," Tom said.

The man frowned. "You're on your feet as much there as here, I suppose. And here, a guy can pick up an extra buck, now and then."

Tapping the till, Tom thought. He said, "I'll trade you, any day." And that was no lie.

Then, outside, a Plymouth convertible was slowing at the curb. He couldn't see who was behind the wheel, but it was Jean's car or a replica.

He rose and said, "My wife. Checking up on me. Stay sober, sport."

As he approached the car, Jean leaned over to open the door on the curb side. She looked worried.

They were moving before she said, "I went past Jud Shallock's house. There's a squad car in front."

"I didn't leave any clues there. That county man probably went to the local police. They may have passed me on the way over."

She kept her eyes on the street ahead. "I wonder what brought the man to Shallock's house? Do you think he had a tip?"

Tom shook his head. "I think it was routine, and then when Jud refused to let the sergeant in, he got suspicious. But if it hits the local paper and that bartender sees it—" Tom paused to stare out the window. "I never should have come back here."

Her voice was low. "No, you should run. That's the standard attitude today. Run from the McCarthy Committee, the Velde Committee and the Gathings Committee. Let freedom die in committee and run for your life. Let the American Hitlers take over."

Tom turned to look at her. He said nothing. He thought, *Migawd, one of those. That's why she came to help me. She's looking for recruits.*

He said, "The murder of my wife wasn't political."

"Of course not. I was speaking of the national attitude. And in case you're wondering about me, I voted Republican since I could vote. I worked actively for General Eisenhower's election."

Tom leaned back against the cushion. "In case you're interested, I *was* wondering about you. You certainly sounded like Moscow Mollie there for a second."

"We'll talk about that, later," she said.

Somewhere, he found a smile, "I'll bet we will. You sounded all wound up, Miss Revolt. You're well named."

"But who's going to wind you up? Who's going to make a fighter out of you?"

"Nobody ever has, Jean. You'd be working stubborn clay. I'm a drifter. I always managed to make a dollar without too much effort and never had to really fight for anything."

"And then you marry an heiress. And then, the one time in your life you should fight, you run." They were on Lincoln Boulevard, now, heading north.

"All right, I should fight," he said. "But why should *you?* Why should *you* get involved in *my* troubles? What am I to you?"

"You are a man who was betrayed by his wife and by his best friend. That friend was my fiancée. I can't fight all the injustice in the world, but I intend to fight all the injustice that touches me."

Tom said nothing.

She said, "You're thinking I should get on a soap box, aren't you?"

Tom shook his head. "No. I was thinking you sound like Joe used to sound. Joe was quite a crusader, too, wasn't he?"

"I always thought he was. Until he sold out. I've been trying to get some of his records from the executor of the estate. I thought there might be a hint there as to who bought Joe." She turned left on Olympic, heading toward the ocean.

They were in the tunnel when she said, "I haven't had any luck, yet. The will hasn't even been read, yet. But Joe didn't have any relatives. And he told me, once, that he was leaving everything to me." She paused. "That would include all his records."

To their left, now, the Pacific was calm in the morning sun. To their right towered the Santa Monica cliff.

"You live out this way?" Joe asked.

"In the Santa Monica Canyon."

That could mean anything. At the ocean end, the area was practically a slum. Farther into the canyon, the property values went soaring.

On Channel Road, she turned right and continued up the canyon to Mesa, where she turned left. This area was now definitely out of the low rent district.

Tom said, "I'll buy that story now about your being a Republican. Though there *are* a few Commies in this town who live high."

She chuckled. "Another joke. That makes two, with that one you pulled in Arizona. You're coming back to life, aren't you?"

"I hope. If an innocent girl can stick her neck out this far for me, I'd be a pretty gutless bastard to run, wouldn't I?"

"In a word, yes."

32

Her house was low, L-shaped, with a shake roof and walls. It wasn't a big house, nor was it a cheap one. It was built on top of a rise and there was a view in all four directions.

She followed the circle of the driveway to the parking area and garage in the rear, and killed the motor.

"Yours?" Tom asked.

"Mine. Bought before prices out here went crazy, I add. Like it?"

"Who wouldn't? And the beach only a few blocks away. You do all right, don't you?"

"Papa did. The magazines were paying him top rates."

Tom closed his eyes. "Revolt? Walter Revolt? The man who wrote all those exposés for the magazines and the press services? He's your father?"

"He was. He died two years ago."

Tom nodded. "I remember, now. One of his series dealt with nationwide gambling tie-ups, if I remember."

"That's right."

Tom turned to face her. "And now you bring a bookie *here*, a bookie convicted of murder."

"Papa would laugh, if he were alive. He had a sense of humor. And if he believed in you as I believe in you, he'd have helped." She opened the door on her side of the car. "Let's not sit here. Unless you intend to run some more. If you do, take the car."

Tom paused only a second before getting out. "The way you talked on the trip, I thought you came from a poor background."

"I *grew up* in a poor background. Dad didn't really hit until about five years before he died. But when he did hit, he appreciated the dollar, and he didn't waste any of them. He bought this place when the invasion scare was at its peak."

Tom nodded. "I remember. Big estates with swimming pools were selling for twelve thousand dollars."

"Mmmm-hmmm. Because people were frightened, people were running. And Dad never ran from anything in his life. Three years later, he was offered five times what he paid for the place."

They went across a bricked patio to a Dutch door, and through that to a farm kitchen, lofty, beamed, one brick wall

33

encasing a high-hearth fireplace.

Tom thought of the showcase Lois had maintained in Beverly Hills, the huge, cold Colonial monstrosity they had shared. He said, "This is the kind of place I wanted but Lois thought it was too California-ish."

Jean smiled. "The phony eastern influence. I thought Lois had more sense. Well, I'll show you your room."

They went through an entrance hall and along a glass-walled passage to a hall serving the bedrooms. The room she showed him to was more like a den, paneled in Philippine mahogany, lined with built-in bookcases.

"It used to be Dad's study," she said. "The windows are low enough for all the light you need but too high for anyone to see in from outside. It seemed like the logical room."

Tom's glance came back to meet hers. "How long did you expect me to live here? Do you realize what you're doing?"

"I know exactly what I'm doing. Once I get Joe's records, we might be able to go to work. Until then, we can compare notes. I've been doing some investigating on my own, you know. That's how I knew about Jud Shallock."

Tom fumbled for his cigarette pack, found it, and offered her one. She took it and he held a light for her. His hand was steady.

"Ready for lunch?" she asked.

"I'm not very hungry. Jean, I've a feeling you're not telling me all you know, your *whole* reason for coming to find me."

"We'll talk about that, too," she said. "Relax, now. You're safer than you've been in days. Relax, while I make some phone calls." She went out.

Tom went over to study a photograph in a leather case which stood on the mantel above the room's small fireplace. It was the face of a man in his fifties, a man with short, dark hair and a blunt nose and a defiant tilt to his jaw.

It was a fighter's face and he recognized it dimly from old newspaper columns. It was her father, undoubtedly.

He heard her voice from the direction of the entrance hall, but couldn't make out what she was saying. He sat in a huge leather chair and leaned back.

A female Don Quixote, in her father's image. A professional bleeding heart. A girl of soap box dialogues and almost

34

soap opera convictions, sticking her neck way out for one of the world's frightened lambs.

And it was such a pretty neck on such a pretty girl. She had so damned much to lose, and what to gain? Unless she'd lost her perspective when Joe Hubbard died. Joe had been a charming gent; he could leave an awful hole in a girl's life.

God damn Joe Hubbard, he thought. *If she's right about him, damn his dirty soul.*

And Lois. . . .?

He closed his eyes, and felt the ache growing behind them. He massaged the back of his neck with a digging hand. He wondered about Jud Shallock, and how he'd fared in the Sheriff's office. And he wondered why he was sitting here, when he could be in Mexico, by now.

He heard a step in the hall and looked up to see her standing in the doorway. "Wouldn't you like a good, stiff drink?"

"I think I would." He straightened in his chair. "Shall I mix us both one?"

"You relax. I'll get them. Bourbon, rye, Scotch?"

"Bourbon and water. That's your dad's picture, there, isn't it?"

She nodded, and went out.

The eyes of Walter Revolt seemed to be fastened on Tom. He closed his own eyes, again, and saw the pinched, rodent-like face of his former cell-mate, Bugs Kiloski.

It was a big-shot's world, was Bugs theme, and he voiced it all during his conscious hours. Bugs had never had a break, by his own admission. He'd been born into poverty and graduated into crime and was now taking the rap because the big boys had let him down. "You can't lick city hall" was a chestnut he savored and "city hall," to Bugs, was any man or group with more brains, money or influence than Bugs had. This included a lot of people.

The sound of a step, again, and Jean was in the room, a pair of drinks in her hands. "Sleeping?"

Tom took the drink she proffered. "Thank you. No, I was thinking of my former cell-mate. He used to claim it was a big-shot's world."

"I guess it always will be. I suppose, in prehistoric times, it was the man with the biggest club or the animal with the

35

sharpest teeth. We've come quite a way from that, though, haven't we?"

"I don't know. This is good whiskey."

She sat in a chair nearby and held her glass aloft. "To success."

They drank to it.

Tom wiped a bead of moisture off his glass with the ball of his thumb. "What's the difference in your mind between a man who runs and a man who accepts a woman for a shield? I think using you in this way is just as contemptible as running."

"I don't. I'm no rabbit, Tom. I worked with my dad on some nasty exposés. I've been threatened quite often."

"Sure. But you're a *woman*. There shouldn't be any doubt in anyone's mind about that. And a woman who has a lot to lose."

She smiled. "Thank you."

He held her gaze. "And you don't even *know* I'm innocent."

"I'm sharing my house with you. If you aren't innocent, why did Joe butcher your case? And then die? And you grew very indignant when I suggested your wife was a tramp. So you didn't know that. And what other reason would you have to kill her?"

He finished his drink. "I had no reason to kill her."

"No. And if you had killed her, you wouldn't be sitting there now. I wouldn't have been able to convince you that you should stop running. If you want to book a bet, I'll bet on you, Tom."

Some of his tension was gone; she'd made him a strong drink. It was quiet, here, and from the mantel, the picture of Walter Revolt seemed to smile at him.

Jean said. "You've already contacted Jud Shallock. Don't look up any more of your old friends, will you?"

"Why not? You don't think they could have had anything to do with it?"

"We don't know, do we? We can't take the chance. You won't, of course, tell Jud you're staying here."

"Of course not. Nor anyone else. But I did want to get in touch with a man named Nannie Koronas. He's got a lot of influence and a lot of money. He can help me."

Jean shook her head. "That's the last man I want you to see. Stay very far away from him."

Chapter 3

SHE'D GONE out to get him another drink. Tom sat there, staring at the picture of Walter Revolt on the mantel. She was her father's daughter, all right; it was the local gambling she was interested in, not Tom Spears.

When she came back, he said, "You've bruised my ego. It's Nannie you're after, isn't it?"

She handed him his drink. "No. It's the killer of Joe Hubbard I'm after. I think your Mr. Koronas knows something about that."

"I see. And all these inspirational sermons to me about making a stand, about not running, were only a pitch to further your own ends."

She stood there rigidly, her eyes cold. "That was rotten, Tom."

"Maybe. If it was, I apologize. And I suppose it's looking a gift horse in the mouth. I apologize again."

She went over to sit on the edge of a chair. She sipped her drink and said nothing.

Tom said, "I don't see any pictures of Joe around."

She didn't look at him. "I burned them. If you want to leave, Tom, I can lend you some money."

"I don't want to leave, Jean. I'm sorry for what I said, really sorry."

Her face was without emotion as she looked at him. "Would you like to nap, now? Or eat?"

"I could nap, I think. This is the first time since I left the clink that I feel completely safe."

She came over to take his glass and he smiled up at her. Her answering smile was brief and cool. "If it's only a nap you want, you can use that blanket that's folded at the foot of the day bed, there."

She went out.

Tom winked at the picture of Walter Revolt and went

37

over to stretch out on the day bed. The security he felt was ridiculous; what could this girl do that the police had failed to do? Granted that a man outside the law would reveal to anyone more than he would to the police, what sources of information could she have, what allies?

If someone in the Koronas organization had killed Joe, Nannie would cover for him, automatically. A group built on the treacherous sands of illegality needed organizational loyalty; Nannie would take care of his own. It might even be why Joe had been killed; perhaps Nannie, too, could evaluate the weakness of the defense Joe had offered.

He lay on the bed and stretched, arching his back, surrendering to the lassitude that was moving through him. Two drinks shouldn't do that. Unless they were doctored. . . .*No, believe in the girl, Tom Spears, or get the hell out of here.*

From somewhere, he heard the sound of water running through pipes and then it grew dimmer and he fell asleep.

He wakened to a dusk-filled room and the distant clack of a typewriter. He was damp with sweat. He had dreamed, but he couldn't remember it now. It must have been a restless sleep; his pillow was on the floor, the bedspread was twisted and dragging. He swung his feet to the floor and sat on the edge of the cot.

The dream came back a little; it had been about Lois and it had involved a bed, a king-sized bed. They'd always argued about that; he had preferred twin beds.

There was a bathroom with a stall shower serving this room. Tom locked the door to the hall and undressed. The clack of the typewriter was constant and beyond it he could hear the sound of traffic on Channel Road. It must be going-home time for the workers who lived out this way. Channel Road didn't carry an audible volume of traffic during normal traffic hours.

There were towels in the bathroom and new bars of soap. There was even a package of three new toothbrushes and an unopened package of razor blades. And talcum and styptic pencil and shaving lotion and Band-aids and aspirin.

All the comforts of home for a killer on the run. Or rather, for a non-killer no longer running.

He had finished his shower, and was shaving, when there

was a knock at the den door.

"Just a moment," Tom called. "I'm naked."

He heard her chuckle.

He slipped on his trousers and went to open the door. "You run a fine hotel, Miss Revolt. But where's the tooth paste?"

"Damn it," she said. "And I was so proud of the way I stocked that bathroom. I did it while you were sleeping."

"I hope I didn't talk in my sleep."

"Not that I heard. I wondered if you were hungry, now?"

"I am. Could I help?"

"No." She gestured toward the bookshelves. "Curl up with a book and I'll call you when dinner's ready. Maybe you had better keep this door locked all the time. I do have friends who like to drop in at odd hours."

He locked the door, after she'd gone back down the hall. He finished his shaving and put on his other shirt and went over to scan the bookcases.

One book was alone on the mantel, and he picked it up. GERANIUM WILDERNESS, by *Jean Revolt*.

The jacket blurb read: *"A penetrating and disturbing view of the fabulous city told with sympathy and wit."* The rear jacket carried a short biographical bit about "this talented daughter of America's beloved latter day Lincoln Steffens, Walter Revolt."

The dedication page read simply: *For Dad.*

An author, too. Her picture on the rear jacket didn't do her justice. Tom took the book back to the big leather chair with him. He was well into it when she knocked again at his door. It was time for dinner.

When he unlocked the door, she was already on her way down the hall again. He followed her to the huge kitchen. The dining table had been moved from its former place near the window. It was now in an ell of the brick wall.

Jean said, "I didn't think it would be bright to have you seated near the window. Even if you're not recognized, it might look a little vulgar at breakfast."

Tom grinned. "We could get married."

She said, "I hope you like lamb chops."

"Love 'em." He sat in the cove of the ell and watched her

39

as she set the hot plates onto the table. "I've been reading your book."

She started to sit down and Tom rose hastily to help her with her chair. Standing above her for that moment, the smell of her perfume came to him and his pulse quickened.

He'd been away from women for too long. She wasn't anything more to him than another woman. He told himself.

When he sat down, again, he said, "I like the way you write."

"Thank you. And do you like what I say?"

"You're your father's daughter, I'd say. I always enjoyed what I read of him. Are you writing another now?"

She nodded. "I sent that first one out under another name. After it had been accepted, my agent revealed my true identity. I didn't want to ride on Dad's reputation."

"Take it from a minor writer, you're not."

She frowned. "A minor writer? You?"

"Mmmm-hmmm. Used to have a handicapping column in the *Blade*."

She chuckled. "You amaze me. Joe used to talk about you a lot." She looked at her plate. "He said you belonged in a better business."

"Better than four hundred dollars a week?"

"You made that much money?"

"I did, for four years."

"Are you going back to it?"

He shook his head. "They frown on that sort of thing in the clink. These are mighty fine chops, lady."

"Don't talk that way." Her voice was sharp.

Startled, he looked up. "About the chops, you mean? Or about the clink?"

"About going back to jail. You're not. And you're not going to run. You're going to be free and clean, when we've finished."

He lifted his water tumbler. "All right, Champ. I'll drink to that."

They drank. They ate in silence for a while. Finally, she asked,"Do the others make four hundred dollars a week, too? The other—lower echelon bookies?"

He shook his head. "I was an upper class agent, remember. My wife had a lot of wealthy friends." He studied her. "And as long as this is the question hour, I've a few, myself."

She said nothing, waiting.

He said quietly, "How did you know about Chuck, in St. Louis? And about Jud Shallock? What are your sources of information?"

"One source," she said, "a man I don't care to name, a private investigator who did a lot of work for Dad."

He shook his head sadly. "A shamus, Lordy! So he knows you were interested in me. And he knows the police are looking for me. There isn't a private investigator in town who won't sell out if he gets his price. Didn't you know that?"

"No. And it's not true. It's one of the beliefs, one of the fallacies all—well—"

He smiled. "All *criminals* believe?"

She faced him candidly. "All people outside of the law."

"Do you? You're outside of the law, right now?"

She made a face. "I'm on the side of the angels." She poured him another cup of coffee. "This man has been offered all kinds of bribes when he worked with Dad. And never succumbed. We won't have to worry about him. It's *your* friends I'm afraid of."

"Shallock?" He shook his head. "Nor Chuck, either. They're solid organization men."

"That's what I mean. They work for Koronas."

That, again. Tom sipped his coffee and said nothing. She was too pretty to qualify as a female crusader; what grudge did she bear Nannie?

"I baked a pie," she said. "Could you eat a piece?"

"Not now. That was a fine meal, and filling. I wonder what's happened to Jud? I wonder if the Sheriff's Department is still holding him."

"Why don't you phone him?"

"The call could be traced. They'll be waiting for me to get in touch with Jud."

"You could call him from a phone booth. Or no, I'll have my investigator find out for you. Until we get those records of Joe's, we aren't going to make *any* moves."

41

Outside, it was now dark and the traffic on Channel had diminished. Across the table from him, Jean looked quietly pensive.

Tom said, "I *am* a problem, aren't I?"

Her smile was dim. "A problem but not a burden. Do you like Stan Kenton?"

"I don't understand him, but I'll listen, with a drink in my hand. I'm more for Dixie."

"I've some of that, too. I've a player that will go all day. And the drinks are in the living room."

Simple enough, clean enough. A pair of betrayed lambs in the dim living room, nursing their drinks and perhaps nursing their private thoughts while the player went from Kenton to Gillespie and then back through time to the boys Tom loved. Fats and Satchmo and Bunny, sentimental communication at his level.

Perhaps nursing their private thoughts but no situation is static. In Tom, the awareness grew. He'd been behind the walls and he was a whole man. And his wife was dead. And Jean's lover was dead and she was all woman, and wasn't writing a sublimation of the sexual drive? She wrote.

The clean full tone of Benny's clarinet rode triumphantly through the room.

Jean said, "This we can both share. What are you thinking of?"

"You." He looked at her. "You're attractive and I'm human, and if that sounds vulgar, forget it."

She smiled. "Christopher Isherwood said what he liked about this canyon was its odor of decay. Perhaps it's that. You're attractive, and I'm human, too. And with another drink, I'd match your vulgarity. This much we have, it isn't infidelity, not with both of them dead."

His body was tight, the hammering of his heart heavy. He tried to keep his face composed. "But you'd need another drink?"

"I'd need another drink. To drown the memory of a man." She looked at him challengingly. "Another drink would do it. Will you mix it?"

Lois had been good, but Jean was better. Lois' body had been beautiful, Jean's was firmer, stronger, more challenging.

42

At the flesh level, it was perfect communication.

And it must have had some significance beyond the flesh level. For the ice he'd lived with since Lois' death was now melted. He cried for five minutes.

In the big dim room, in the quiet night air lightly touched with her fragrance, peace came to him. He reached over to take her hand.

"Sentimentalist," she said. "I suspected it. I'm glad. We were good together. But that's not enough and you're also enough of a realist to appreciate that." A pause. "I hope."

"Don't talk," he said. "You're trained to think words will do anything. *But don't talk, now.*"

Quiet; the sound of an occasional car going by on Channel or Entrada, her hand quiescent in his. If this had been a transient urge, he could not feel tenderness for her now. But he did.

Watch it, Tom Spears, he told himself. *You are a hunted man, a convicted killer. Don't drag her into the dust with you.*

"Maybe," she said quietly, "it was a thing we both needed. Therapeutic, you know? No significance. I'm sorry—you told me not to talk."

"We can talk. What amazes me is that we hadn't met oftener. I knew Joe very well. We spent a lot of time together. And you were his fiancée—"

"He lived in two worlds. Despite your wealthy wife, you were in his other world. Do you doubt me, Tom?" She withdrew her hand.

"No. Are you hungry? I could use a sandwich."

She chuckled. "Beast." She rose to a sitting position, and the fine, firm silhouette of the upper half of her body was revealed by the dim light from the hall. "Ham, corned beef, salami?"

"Surprise me. You're an ace, Jean Revolt."

"Quit talking like Zane Gray. And get up; you'll get no meals in bed in *this* house."

He rose, to fumble for his trousers, as she slipped into a robe and left the room. When he came out to the kitchen, she was preparing a sandwich by the dim illumination of the stove light.

She said, "This room has too many windows and it faces

on the driveway. Perhaps you'd better wait in the living room."

He was just leaving the kitchen, when the headlights flashed in the drive.

"Your room, quickly," Jean said. "It's probably some of my whimsical friends. They drop in at all hours. Hurry!"

Tom was already racing down the hall, the momentary illusion of security gone, the urge to flight again in full command. In the paneled room, he closed and bolted the door. Then he stood with his back pressed to it, trembling.

He heard the sound of the door chime and then the clack of Jean's mules on the kitchen linoleum. He couldn't hear the front door open, but he heard the voices, festive voices, unnecessarily loud, tinged with alcoholic overtones.

Just friends, drunken friends, cruising the night and looking for a friendly light. Tom took a deep breath and relaxed against the door.

And then he remembered that most of the clothes he'd worn were still in Jean's bedroom. And one of the bathrooms led off that room. He stood quietly by the door trying to hear the conversation that was now going on in the entrance hall.

Jean was saying, "I don't like to be rude, but I am tired. It's been a horrible day."

A male voice said, "Just a night cap is all, just a touch of warmth for the road."

Silence, and then Jean said, "All right. A little one. I'm too weary to mix it. I guess you can handle that, Dick."

"And I," a masculine voice said, "would like to use one of your smaller rooms. The one off the study available?"

"No," Jean said quickly, "the plumbing is jammed up in there. Use the one off my bedroom."

Great. . . . There would be no reason for the gent to assume the clothes belonged to Tom Spears. But there would be sufficient reason for him to assume the obvious. Well, maybe in her circle, this was standard operating procedure. Though he didn't want to think so.

And why didn't he?

He stayed near the door, a fine sweat forming on his body. The chatter from the kitchen was lower, now, indistinguishable. There was the sound of water moving through pipes.

Then, less than a minute later, there were footsteps in the hall outside, footsteps that paused and then came his way. And then he had the feeling that someone was standing just inches away from him on the other side of the door.

Tom stopped breathing, and the pound of his heart seemed to be audible. He heard a rasp at waist level and knew the person out there was trying the door. The knob turned, but the bolt held the door fast. In a few seconds, footsteps went up the hall toward the kitchen.

Just friends cruising the night and looking for a friendly light . . . ? Not this one. A nose, this one. Looking for a tidbit of scandal? Or maybe something more. Tom pressed his ear to the door, waiting for the nosy one to make some remark to his hostess.

He heard nothing; the conversation murmur continued but there were no words he could distinguish. He stayed there, next to the door, until they'd left.

Silence after the grind of the starter and the diminishing throb of the motor. A knock, and he opened the door.

Jean still wore nothing but the robe. "Just friends," she said. She exhaled. "Butterflies."

"Which one went to the growler as soon as he came in?"

She stared at him in the dimness. "Why?"

"Because, after he left the bathroom, he tried this door. Some of my clothes are still in your room, remember."

"Lordy, I'd forgotten." She looked up at him and smiled. "There goes my fine reputation. Though these aren't the kind of people who'd make a production of it. Still hungry? We could have our sandwich now."

"Don't be so unconcerned, Jean. Who was the man?"

"His name is Ames Gilchrist. Know him?"

Tom shook his head. "But it was still a surprising thing for him to do, trying that knob, wasn't it?"

"Not if you knew Ames. I suspect he carries pornographic postcards in his pocket. Let's eat; I'm starved."

The sandwich she'd started for him was still there, and there was still some coffee in the pot. They ate quietly in the dark kitchen, lighted only indirectly by the overflow from the living room.

Jean was quiet, and she didn't seem disturbed, and Tom

45

wondered at the poise that could go through the emotional disturbances of this day.

He said quietly, "You're pretty well disciplined, emotionally, aren't you?"

"When I need to be. When it's important to be. Dad taught me that." She smiled. "Was I, an hour or so ago?"

He looked at the tablecloth.

She chuckled. "I'm sorry. I've tried to discipline myself against fear, against running from trouble that needs to be met. Is that wrong? Is that cold?"

"No. How about a piece of that apple pie you baked for dinner?"

"Damn you." Her laugh was light. "And *you* call *me* disciplined."

Chapter 4

HE COULDN'T sleep. Perhaps it was because of the afternoon nap, but he lay with open eyes in the locked, dark study that had served Walter Revolt. He thought back to St. Louis, to the finding of Lois' body. He went back to the days before that, the great days of their marriage and their friendship with Joe Hubbard.

It simply didn't add. Joe had been a friend, friend, *friend*. He couldn't be that wrong about Joe. And how often he and Lois had seen Joe. And he couldn't remember any meeting with Jean except for that one in the office. Had Joe been ashamed of her?

Or had Joe been ashamed of them, of him and Lois? Or had Joe and Lois, perhaps, been. . . . *Watch it, Tom Spears, you're really reaching, now.*

Well, why not? Think anything you please; your neck's involved, and if the improbable can give you a lead, stay with it.

All right, then, Joe and Lois. And when Lois was killed, Joe's conscience insisted he come to St. Louis to handle the defense of his friend. Logical enough—but why was Joe killed?

Jean said that Joe had lived in two worlds. Lois evidently

had, too; one of them the shadow world of infidelity. And hadn't he, too, with his wife's friends in one and the organization of Nannie Koronas comprising the other?

And Jean, crusading daughter of a crusader, who also knew some butterflies? Jean, in bed, was not the poised and determined Jean who had searched the desert for him. All four of them had some Jekyll-Hyde facets.

There might be something in an extension of that thought; a hunch gnawed at him and went away without identification.

He thought of Jud Shallock who had only one face, so far as he knew. He wondered about Jud and if the County men were giving him a bad time.

Two loyal friends he had, two who had given him sanctuary, Jud Shallock and Jean Revolt. On this pleasant thought, he fell asleep.

Early in the morning, he wakened, the sheet beneath him damp with his perspiration. There'd been a dream, now only half remembered, a dream involving cops and a narrowing circle and the putty-white dead face of his wife.

Outside the high window over his head, a bird sang. From the air high above, the muted sound of a big plane came to him, one of the big birds, coming in across the Pacific. From where? From any of a number of places he might run to, given the money and the phony identification.

Nannie could take care of both of those. Nannie Koronas had the money and the connections. Stay away from Nannie, Jean had warned him. But Nannie took care of his own; it was a rule he lived by. And Tom was one of Nannie's boys.

From the direction of the Coast Highway came the rumble of the big Diesel trucks, out early to beat the jam of work-time traffic. Outside his window, there were two birds, now, greeting the morning in a pleasantly discordant duet.

He swung out of bed and the morning air was cool on his damp body. He took a leisurely, warm shower and then wrapped one of the huge towels around him and shaved carefully and slowly.

He was, he reflected, as he studied his image, no longer running. But neither was he doing anything else. Unless accepting the sanctuary of a dedicated female could be called doing something.

47

When he went out, later, into the hall, he could see her in the kitchen, squeezing some oranges with a hand juicer. Her short dark hair was tousled, still. She was wearing a halter and shorts and her tanned, slim body quickened his pulse.

She looked up as he entered the kitchen, her clear blue eyes resting thoughtfully on his face. "Something's on your mind."

"Inaction. I'm a man who likes to wheel and deal."

"We will. Patience. Eggs this morning?"

"Scrambled."

"Bacon?"

"Thank you, yes." He sat at the end of the table protected from outside view by the brick wall. "Can I help?"

She shook her head. "Men always sit down *before* they ask if they can help." She sniffed. "Why?"

"I don't know. And why are you dressed so charmingly and revealingly this morning?"

She turned to look at him. "Because the weather man assures us it's going to be hot, a scorcher. Why else?" Her eyes probed his unflinchingly.

He felt himself color faintly. "I—Uh, sorry—"

She smiled. "You're blushing. You're not a complete beast. You're blushing. So I'll admit I *might* have thought of you when I put this on." She brought him a small glass of orange juice.

"Bring yours and sit down," he told her. "I'll handle the eggs."

She brought her glass over and sat across from him. She said, "My investigator is coming today, this morning. You won't need to hide."

"He knows I'm here?"

She nodded.

Some tenseness moved through Tom. He had a feeling of being manipulated, a momentary sense of puppetry. He rose and went to the stove.

She said, "I'll take them scrambled, too. You don't completely trust me, do you, Tom?"

He turned the flame low under the griddle. "I trust your intentions. You're playing what could be a disastrous game."

"I know that."

48

He cracked some eggs into a bowl. "And why? They're both dead. And what am I to you?"

"A lamb. And the word around town is that you're—what the boys call—an ace."

"That's not enough." He added a touch of cream to the eggs.

"It's enough for me." Her voice was quieter. "And for lagniappe, we have last night."

A pause, a moment's meaningful silence, and he asked, "How many strips of bacon?"

Her laugh was low and mocking.

The investigator came at ten-thirty. His name was Leonard Delavan and he was a man of about forty-five, a stocky man with a square, intelligent face. His hair was gray and cut short. It gave the block face a pugnacious look.

In the living room, as they were being introduced, Jean said, "Leonard has had seven years with the FBI and four with Naval Intelligence. He is not what *you* might contemptuously consider a '*shamus*'."

His own word, she was throwing at him. Tom smiled and shook Leonard Delavan's hand. And as Delavan smiled, Tom saw a quick, transient resemblance to the picture of Walter Revolt.

Delavan said evenly, "You have the most to lose in this operation, Tom. But you also stand to gain the most. Neither Jean nor I have anything to gain, personally." He took a breath. "And our necks to lose. We're all outside the law, I guess you realize."

Tom nodded. "I do."

They went back to the study. There, Delavan said slowly, "I've been investigating your wife's—background." He studied Tom. "She was a—busy woman."

Tom nodded. "I'm beginning to learn that."

Delavan continued to study him. "*Insatiable* might be the word."

Tom took a deep breath. Outside, the bird still sang. He asked quietly, "How sure are you?"

Delavan shrugged. "I never followed her, personally. As

49

sure as a man can be who is trained to examine evidence and evaluate witnesses. The gist of it makes you out a pretty sad patsy."

Tom said nothing. Resentment was moving through him, resentment at this invasion of his privacy, but he stilled it. He sat on the unmade studio bed.

Delavan said, "One of her lovers was Joe Hubbard."

Jean's quick intake of breath rasped through the room. Tom turned to look at her and then looked back dully at the detective. He said calmly, "I was thinking of that possibility last night." He looked at Jean. "*Late*, last night, after those people left."

Jean sat down in the big chair, staring at him.

Delavan said, "That might account for the miserable defense Joe put up for your life. But it doesn't account for Joe's death, at least not directly. Incidentally, Joe Hubbard's death strengthens your position. Because you were in jail, when he died. And it would need one hell of a belief in coincidence to assume his death and your wife's weren't connected in some way."

"It couldn't have been suicide?"

Delavan frowned. "No. What made you think of that?"

"I was thinking that Joe had a conscience. It might not look like it from where we stand, now, but I'm sure he did."

In the big chair, Jean nodded. "I'll accept that. It might give us a lead, too."

Delavan shrugged. "Maybe, but that's theory. I think, though, we're getting Joe's papers. That could give us a more definite lead. I've a date with his executor at one o'clock."

Jean said, "We'll be waiting for you, here. And what else have you learned? What about Jud Shallock?"

"He was released." Delavan looked at Tom. "You didn't leave any signs of occupancy behind, fortunately, and the police seem to feel Shallock's in the clear. He's safe enough."

"From the police, anyway," Jean said. "All right, Leonard, we'll wait for those papers." She rose, and went to the door with him.

When Jean came back, she said, "I'm going out in the back for a sunning. I've locked the front door and perhaps you'd better lock this one. I'll hear any bells."

"Okay. I'll finish your book." He paused. "Do you believe that story about Joe and Lois?"

"Why not? One corruption is all corruption. Keep this door locked."

"Sure. Doesn't it bother you—about Joe and Lois?"

She stared at him a moment without answering. Then she went out and closed the door quietly behind her.

He sat there for seconds before rising to lock the door and get her book.

She composed a readable and interesting prose; he stayed with the book right through to the end, in complete communication all the way. He understood her a little better, now, a girl brought up in the nasty section of this town, a girl of sensitivity and courage who didn't know how the better half lived until five or six years before her father's death.

A knock, and her voice. "Ready for lunch?"

He went to open the door. "Any time. I've finished your book. I like you."

This time, it was her turn to blush. "Thank you. It wasn't completely autobiographical." She turned, and had started down the hall, when the sound of the siren came.

Tom had started to follow, but he paused as she turned. Her voice was steady. "Easy. There are sirens all the time on the Coast Highway."

Tom nodded. They stood there, unmoving, waiting for another sound. Then Jean indicated with a gesture that he should stay where he was. She went down the hall to the kitchen.

Tom didn't take his eyes from her as she stood by the sink, looking out the window that revealed the parking area.

Then, as he dimly heard the sound of a car coming up the grade, she turned and said, "Get in the room. Lock the door."

He knew at that moment, somehow, that the room was no longer a sanctuary. He put on his jacket and had picked up his extra shirt before the chime sounded.

He was back at the door in time to hear her opening, "Yes?"

The voice of the man at the door was too low for him to hear, but he heard Jean's, "I don't quite understand. You're looking for someone?"

A mumble, and then Jean's, "You've brought a warrant, a search warrant, I suppose? You have? Well, in that case—"

Tom didn't wait to hear more. He pulled a chair over to the high window near his bed and climbed up on it. He slid the window open and looked out.

There was a gully behind the house, here, and the drop was certainly enough to break an ankle, or worse. But a future much worse than anything the gully might offer was personified in that cop at the door. He was never going back to that place.

He stuffed his shirt into his jacket pocket and threw a leg over the sill. He didn't look down, again. There were some shrubs lining the walls of the gully; the position he intended to drop from would land him directly over one of them. How strong the roots were, how much his passing grasp would break the fall were things he couldn't know until he'd dropped. All he knew now was that the gray walls were closing in, again.

He pulled the other leg out and swung around, gripping the slanting edge of the sill. Then his legs were free and dangling and his fingers were slipping from the sill. He held his breath and managed by an effort of will, to keep his eyes open as his fingers left the edge.

There was the slap of the shrub on his legs and he grabbed out blindly. The leaves came off in his hand and he grasped desperately at the thickest bough in sight. He had a grip on it momentarily and his body swung in an arc.

And then his knee smashed into an outcropping of rock and the fierce pain of it screamed through his brain. His hands loosened on the bough and he dropped the rest of the way, nausea surging in him, his aching knee half bent in a hopeful attempt to prevent its taking the impact of his fall.

There was a jar in his uninjured leg and then he went head over heels down the last few feet of the fall. He lay there a moment, the breath knocked out of him, a boulder that could have meant his finish not three feet from his blurred vision.

He was alive, he was conscious. And nothing, he was sure, was broken. His bruised knee throbbed steadily and there was the bitterness of vomit in his mouth. But he was alive—and out of the house now being searched for him.

52

He had to get up. The grass was tall enough here to make crawling an adequate camouflage if his pursuers were on the ground. But viewed from above, the grass was no cover. And it was hot, today, and he knew what rattlesnakes remained in this gully would be out.

A snake bite below waist level was not nearly as dangerous as one above; he had to get to his feet. He took a deep breath and put a tentative hand out toward the boulder for support. He rose, his weight centered on his left leg. He looked up and saw that the open window above was still devoid of any searching eyes.

Gingerly, he tried to shift his weight to his injured right leg. Nausea stirred in him, again, and the aching knee seemed to expand until the pain ran from his hip to his ankle.

He took another deep gulp of the hot, clean air and tried to flex the knee slightly. His mouth was dry as the gray grass around him as he turned to consider the quickest way to concealment in the gully.

There was no bend in it, no cover in either direction; he started limping painfully down the slight grade that must lead to the sea.

Still, no face had appeared in the window. Jean had undoubtedly shown the policeman every room in the house as slowly as possible until he had demanded entrance into the locked study. And there, she could have stalled for more time, pretending to search for a key.

There would be no doubt, probably, in the policeman's mind that the room had been occupied last night. But there would be no proof the occupant had been Tom Spears. Probably. He hoped.

And who had tipped off the police? What had brought them there? Jud didn't know he was there. Could it have been Delavan? That seemed unlikely. The door-knob-tryer of last night? What was his name—? Gilchrist, Ames Gilchrist.

That wouldn't make too much sense. If he was the kind of person Jean had suggested, wouldn't he have tried a spot of blackmail first? Unless there was a reward.

Any of Jean's friends would know she'd been engaged to Joe Hubbard and any who could read would know Joe Hubbard had defended him—and then been killed. So, if Gilchrist

53

wanted to add the possibles but improbables, he might guess that the occupant of the locked room was Tom Spears. But it was a big improbable.

The fine sweat of pain and apprehension was soaking through his shirt, now, trickling down his legs. If this grade led to the sea, it meant opening onto the Coast Highway. And he remembered no gully in the cliff along the highway here, except for the Santa Monica Canyon.

It couldn't finish at the highway; it must come out somewhere along Channel Road or else cut off into lower, level ground out of sight of the highway.

Despite the fact there had been no turning, the overhang above now concealed him from view of the house. He was out of sight.

But it was only temporary. A chair under an open window in a room that had been locked; any person over three years old would know where to look next.

The ache was constant in his right leg, but he limped on steadily and now there was a turn in the gully ahead and he heard the sound of motor traffic to his left.

He came to the turn and saw ahead the rear of a two story, frame building and next to that a littered, empty, macadam parking lot. The lot wasn't completely empty; an antiquated and deserted Buick gathered dust in the nearest corner.

There was a chain across the entrance to the lot. There was probably not enough business to make it a going proposition during the week; it depended on the week-end beach trade.

He stood in the ell of the gully, watching the traffic going by on Channel. He hesitated coming out into the view of all those passing, but the only other course was back the way he had come. And he had no time to waste.

He took a deep breath and limped out boldly into the sunlight of the parking lot, his gaze missing nothing, searching for the blue of a uniform or the insignia of a Department car.

The haven of the deserted Buick occurred to him; the rear doors were intact and the windows dark with grime. But if the canyon was searched, the Buick would not be overlooked. He forced himself to walk past its beckoning concealment.

Slowly, he moved past the side of the two-story building and then he heard the bark of a big motor and saw a bus angling toward the curb directly ahead.

He waved and tried to quicken his pace, biting his lower lip against the increasing pain from his swelling knee. The lone waiting passenger had entered and the door was closing by the time Tom made the sidewalk.

The exhaust rumble rose, preparatory to departure and Tom was shouting. The bus was half out into the traffic zone and he had slowed to a walk when the bus driver looked back. He stopped the monster, and the folding doors swung open.

Swinging his bad leg up to the level of the first step brought quick tears to his eyes and the bus driver's curious glance rested a moment on Tom's sweating face.

"First time I've gone without the crutch," Tom said. "I should have had more sense."

The driver's eyes showed no concern; they shifted to the cash box, waiting for the fare. Tom deposited it and walked back through the mildly curious glances to a seat in the rear.

He learned, there, he couldn't sit down without putting his right leg awkwardly out into the aisle. The puffed knee would not bend enough to give him clearance from the seat ahead. He stood.

He tried to look casual, to inspect the other passengers without interest, as the bus swung out onto the Coast Highway and turned left. He hadn't been able to see the sign on front; it was just luck he'd picked one heading for Santa Monica. The other way led to the Palisades, and that was no hamlet for a stranger.

The passengers were standard enough, shoppers and a few giggling teen-agers making a nuisance of themselves in the wide rear seat. Not a man who looked like a cop among the dozen or so passengers.

Get out of town, he told himself. And her voice came back in his memory, "This is no time to run. This is a time to make a stand."

That it might be—if you were clean. He wasn't. He had been convicted of murder and he was evading what they called justice, right now. Justice is a word that means legality to the law. It meant a number of things to a number of people,

55

but the men who made and enforced the laws had a single interpretation of it, codified in their dusty books.

He had to take care of his own justice; he was no longer one of the upright citizens. He meant to live, even if it was on his knees. He meant to live any way he could so long as it was outside the walls.

On Santa Monica Boulevard, in Santa Monica, he got off the bus and stood a moment in the bright sunlight, pretending to look for an address.

Only Beverly Hills was policed better than this town; it was no city for a man on the run.

But to the south of this Rotarian's roosting ground sprawled Venice, a tangled waterside litter of shacks and cramped apartments housing the unwashed and the unwanted.

He knew a few of the unwanted in Venice and here was the red bus coming down the boulevard. He swung the good left leg aboard and brought the rest of his aching body in awkwardly. The driver waited in indifferent patience; the driver wasn't surprised at anything on the Venice run.

"First day without the crutch," Tom explained.

The driver swung the door control lever and headed out into the traffic. He was paid to carry fares, not make conversation.

It was an old bus and the noxious bite of carbon monoxide stirred the nausea in Tom as he went limping down the aisle, examining each passenger in turn.

There were only six or seven and each of them looked innocent enough. At the back, he sat on the wide seat, his stiff leg in the aisle.

Who would be safest in Venice? He knew a bookie there and a couple of poverty-stricken horse players. And then his memory went groping, and he remembered a girl.

He and Joe, out on the town one night and very drunk. And Joe knew a girl who would have a friend and she was the kind of girl you could drop in on any time of the night. They'd dropped in and the girl had called a friend and it had been one hell of a night, an orgy.

He couldn't think of it with complete distaste; nothing had happened, he'd been too drunk to be potent. The girl, if he remembered correctly, had been a B girl Joe had represented in court. And he'd saved her from a determined district attorney with some legal shenanigans. Joe had been pleased with the case. And the girl pleased with Joe. Tom remembered the look in her eyes as she'd greeted him.

The girl they'd got for Tom he couldn't remember now, except that she'd been a little heavy for his taste. And the guilt he'd felt when the night was over, though he was still physically unblemished; that he remembered.

But Joe's girl—what had her name been? Carol—? No, it started with a "C." Connie—that was it. Connie, a nickname for Constance. Connie would sound better than Constance in a bar.

He had no idea what her address had been. Nor any reason to believe she hadn't moved. He knew that it was over a garage, and that the inside of the place had surprised him with its apparent taste and sense of warmth.

He remembered he'd wished he and Joe could change partners; Connie had been the kind of busty, leggy blonde to which he was most vulnerable. But she'd had an awful yen for Joe. She was only one of many who lusted for Joe Hubbard, the big bastard.

And one more thing he remembered, her apartment was close to the water. He could see the beach from the bathroom window; one of the living room windows faced out onto a restaurant across the street.

He got off at Windward, and paused a moment looking at all the bars that lined both sides of the street to the ocean. A drink might help, but he couldn't afford to tarry.

He walked south on the street closest to the beach, his eyes seeking the remembered restaurant. Winos dozed in the doorways he passed; a pair of teen-aged hoodlums stared at him insolently as he went by.

What was the name of that restaurant? The ache in his right leg throbbed in unison with his swinging of it; the whole right side of his body seemed to be affected. There was even a soreness in his right eye.

On Venice Boulevard, he paused, surveying the street ahead. What in hell had brought him here? What made him think a girl who'd met him briefly a few years back would offer him any kind of sanctuary now?

57

She was probably no lover of the law, but visiting her, now, would be the brassiest kind of imposition on his part.

Where else could he go? What other haven did he have? And he would pay, once he got hold of some money. She owed Joe enough; he'd saved her from the gray stone walls. And he had been Joe's friend.

But perhaps Joe had been paid again and again. Joe alive had been a king-size Galahad in Tom's mind. Joe dead was being revealed as a big bastard constantly at stud.

Where else to go, though? He walked on, past 23rd and 24th. He could offer to pay for haven and accept her answer. He could make it clear he was buying only a few day's rest until he could get to Nannie for some money.

No other street in the area would have a restaurant and still be close to the water. It would have to be on this street. Ahead, he saw a protruding restaurant sign, swinging over the narrow walk.

He tried to move faster but the pain seeped up from his knee and gagged him. He slowed down, apprehension growing in him. To his right, a narrow, alley-like street led to the beach, and here was an apartment, over a three-car garage. Directly across the street, now, was the restaurant.

The front of the apartment faced on a small, beaten-earth court, he remembered. He walked past the edge of the garage, and there was the gray dust of the court.

There were no taller buildings between here and the sea; the calm water blinked at him in the afternoon's brilliance. He hesitated only a moment before turning and heading for the wooden steps that ran to the small porch above.

There was a pail on the porch, up here, and a string mop. There was a folded, throw-away advertising sheet. There was a card under the bell button.

The card read: *Connie Garrity.*

He took a deep breath and reached for the button.

Chapter 5

HE HEARD the chime sound within, and nothing more. He tried it again and still there was no indication of a response from inside. He stood there quietly, something close to despair welling in his aching body.

And then he turned and saw her coming across the wooden walk through the court, a bag of groceries in the crook of one arm.

She was tanned to a mahogany brown and the bleached hair seemed white against the darkness of her skin. She walked erectly, her long legs moving with a springy vitality. She was dressed in a faded denim sunsuit and doing very well by it.

Just before she got to the foot of the wooden stairs, she looked up. She saw him, there, and paused, a hand on the railing.

"Remember me?" he asked quietly.

Her tan, unlined face went slack in shock. "My God," she said hoarsely. "What—?" She shook her head. "My God."

"I know," he said. "I'll go. You've read the papers, of course. I'll—" He started down the steps.

"Stay where you are," she said. "I'm coming up."

She came up steadily, her eyes on his, surprise on her face but no fear.

When she had reached the porch, Tom said, "I remembered you as a friend of Joe's. I'm hotter than hell, I guess you know."

"I guess I do." She had her key in her hand now, and was opening the door. "You'd better get in here, and quick."

She shoved the door open and stood aside for him to enter first. "Hurry."

He came into a fairly large kitchen he dimly remembered, of blue with an upholstered breakfast nook in the corner nearest the door.

Tom sat on the edge of the upholstered bench, his bad leg out stiffly in front of him. She put the bag of groceries

59

on the table and considered him gravely.

Tom said, "This was awful damned brassie, but—" He shrugged.

She said, "Any port in a storm, sailor. Did you kill her, Tom Spears?"

He looked at her dully, shaking his head. "No, and I don't know who killed her. Nor who killed Joe Hubbard, but that they couldn't pin on me; I was in jail at the time."

"I know." She looked at his stiff leg. "What's wrong with that?"

"I bruised my knee—getting away from a—a place I was hiding. You must think I'm some bastard, running to you, a girl I don't even know. You can throw me out, any time."

She came around the end of the table. "We discussed that. Take your pants off. I want to see that knee."

He must have colored, for she laughed. "Lord, what a time for modesty. Get 'em off, impotent; I've had some nurse's training." She bent, to pull at his cuffs.

He said stiffly. "If your friend told you I was impotent, she lied. I was drunk, is all."

She laughed, and Tom smiled, realizing the absurdity of it. He loosened his belt and opened his fly and she pulled his trousers gently from the bottom, sliding them along the floor.

The knee was big as a sugar melon, the skin taut and discolored.

"Football knee," she said. "Ripped cartilage, I'd bet a nickel." She looked up. "How far did you come on it?"

"I came by bus, most of the way. If it is a football knee, I guess it's a good thing I kept working it, right? How sure are you?"

"Fairly sure. Your face is filthy; did you know that? You look like a refugee from Windward Avenue. Well, you're in the area for it. What happened to Joe, Tom?"

"I don't know. I don't know anything. A—a friend of mine and—I mean a friend of Joe's and I were going to work on it, but then the law came, and I had to run. I don't know why I thought of you, except I wanted to get out of Santa Monica, and—"

"Take it easy," she interrupted. "And stop being so damned

apologetic. If you're a killer, you're the first killer lamb I've ever met. You don't even make a good adulterer."

He leaned back against the padding of the bench. "I could use a tall, cold glass of water. You're wonderful, Connie."

"Mmmm-hmmm." She went to the refrigerator and brought out a bottle of spring water. She filled a glass and brought it to him. "Joe used to say I was wonderful. But he probably told all his girls that. Including that bleeding heart who liked to think she was engaged to him."

Tom frowned. "You mean that—what was her name—Revolt, wasn't it?"

"Mmmm-hmmm. Jean Revolt. Her daddy was the big newspaper guy. Remember?"

"Oh, yes. Walter Revolt. I think I met Jean once, in Joe's office."

Connie refilled his glass. "That was Joe's canyon cutie. Then he had one in Hollywood and one in Studio City and down here in lowly Venice, he had Connie Garrity. Joe was quite an operator. Covered this town like a blanket. Or a sheet, I should say. Well, I'm not bitter. *I'm* still alive."

Tom said quietly, "I guess he had another one, too. In Beverly Hills."

"No doubt." She paused, staring at him. "Wait—you lived in Beverly Hills."

He nodded. "So did my wife."

She was silent for seconds. Then, "No. Oh, Tom, no—! How many times did he tell me you were his best friend? Oh, this I can't buy, Tom Spears. This is—Oh, that *miserable bastard!*"

"Great personality," Tom said. "Charm coming out of his ears. Great fighter for the rights of man, great shining-haired crusader, a super-charged Don Quixote."

She sat down on the bench opposite, staring at him. "Take it easy, he's dead. He wasn't the only one of his kind, we have to remember. He could have had plenty of integrity away from bed."

"Maybe. But I've been told, since, that he mishandled the trial. I've been assured by experts that for a lawyer of his ability, he must have mishandled it intentionally."

Silence, for seconds, in the blue kitchen, and then she

61

said, "I've heard that rumor, myself. A girl hears all kinds of things in bars, though."

Tom said nothing.

Connie reached over to get a glass from the drainboard behind her. Slowly, she poured herself a glass of water. Her hand shook a little.

She said softly, "One of the men who told me Joe had butchered the case should know. He's a top criminal lawyer. I guess that wouldn't qualify as ordinary bar talk." She sipped her water. "You don't think Joe killed your wife, do you?"

Tom shrugged.

Connie's voice was quiet. "He didn't. We read about the murder, over the breakfast table, here. Joe was horribly shocked."

Tom's gaze went from the bleached hair of Connie Garrity to the soft brown eyes, looking strangely vulnerable in that taut face. He said, "Joe's dead and I'm sorry I've learned all I have. I'd rather remember him the way I knew him."

She looked at the table top. "To hell with him. But what about you? You're not dead. You'll need money, I suppose?" She looked up.

"I think I can get some. I wonder if the police will think of looking for me here."

"Not unless they can trace your movements. Nobody knows about me and Joe, nobody but us."

"And that girl who was here, that night?"

"She went back to Milwaukee."

Tom rubbed his knee tenderly, staring at the floor.

"You'd better get into a hot tub," she said. "I'm not working tonight. We'll think of something after your bath. Soak that knee in water as hot as you can stand."

Tom didn't stir. "No. I think it will be better for both of us if I just phone a friend and have him pick me up here. There isn't any reason in the world why I should implicate you in my troubles."

"They'll be watching your friends. C'mon, I'll get the tub filled for you. This is the safest place you could be, Tom." She stood up. "This is probably the least policed area west of the Rockies." She went through the doorway to the living room and a little later there was the sound of running water.

The phone was here in the kitchen and Tom stared at it, thinking of Nannie. Jean had told him to stay away from Nannie, but Jean had her personal reasons for that.

Tom rose painfully and went over toward the phone. He was just reaching for it, when Connie said from the doorway, "*No.* I don't want any of your friends to know you're here. You won't blame me if I don't trust your friends?"

"They're not all like Joe," Tom said. "I was going to call the boss."

"The boss—?"

"The big man. I was a bookie, you know."

"I know. I don't want any big men to know you're here. If you stay here, it's under my conditions. And I want you to stay until we can figure something. You bring out the maternal in me."

Tom expelled his breath. The weariness of his flight and his pain was bone-deep now; he stared at her dully.

"Come on, lamb," she said gently. "I'll scrub your back."

It wasn't only the knee that was battered. He had a bruise as big as his hand, a nasty blue-black discoloration above his right hip.

When he was dry, she gave him a robe to wear and it figured that she would have a man's robe around the house; she didn't bother to explain why, which figured, too.

When he came out into the living room, she was relaxed in a huge, chartreuse chair, a frosted glass in her hand. She smiled amiably, "The stuff's on the kitchen drainboard if you want one. Tom Collins."

Tom shook his head. "Not now, thanks. Why do women want to protect me? I must be a perpetual adolescent."

"I just like a man around the house," she answered. "I don't feel whole without a man around the house." She sipped her drink and regarded him. "This place you ran from— this place you ruined the knee running from—was that a woman's place, too?"

He started to shake his head, but paused. He made no gesture.

"All right," she said, "it was. I won't ask you her name. Why don't you lie on the davenport, Tom? You're safe here."

He sat on the davenport, his back supported by one end. "I thought I was safe, there, too. I mean the place I just left. I might have been; it could have been a routine check. *But the man brought a warrant.* I can't understand it. There was no way to connect us."

"There must have been one way. And that could be a help, that could be a lead as to who killed them both." She finished her drink. "But we're not detectives, are we? And we don't want to play detective, do we? We're brighter than that." She stood up. "I'll mix you a weak one." She started toward the kitchen.

"Wait—" Tom said, and she turned. "I was thinking," he went on, "that you made a good point there. And I was wondering if maybe what you know about Joe and what—" He paused, suddenly realizing *that* had been a revelation.

She smiled. "Oh, a girl? A girl who knew Joe? I won't guess. It would be too obvious. I'll get your drink."

When she came back from the kitchen, she had a pair of drinks in her hands. She handed him one. "No more palaver, Tom, about what she knows and I know. I never fight city hall."

Tom smiled. "That's what my cell-mate used to say— 'you can't lick city hall.' The knowledge didn't keep him out of jail."

She relaxed again in the chartreuse chair. "It's kept me out. You know, I watched this Un-American Activities Committee on TV. I couldn't feel sorry for a single one of those unfriendly witnesses. You think I'd make a fight for people like that?"

Tom studied her. "What brought that up? What's that got to do with me, and Joe?"

"Nothing." She put the cool glass to her forehead. "I wasn't talking about you and Joe. I was talking about the un-named girl you just left."

"You think she's a Commie?"

"I know she isn't. Joe told me she isn't. But so many of her friends were, *by some chance.* Joe and I used to laugh about her; tell her that next time you see her. She's a hang-over from the days when women were fighting for their rights. She's trying to be her old man—with skirts."

64

"You got her wrong," Tom said. "Believe me, Connie, you got her *way* wrong. She's a great girl."

"Sure, maybe you weren't impotent around her, eh? Lambie, don't feed me any malarky on the girl. I saw her through *Joe's* mind. And whatever we now think about that big bastard, he had a lot of mind, and he used it. Could we drop the subject?"

"Sure." Tom sipped his drink, and it was weak. But cooling. "Sure—if it bothers you. Jealousy?" His smile was slight. "Joe *did* call her his fiancée."

"Why not? It didn't cost him anything. I don't want to talk about her, Tom. I don't enjoy being nasty."

"All right. And I don't want to talk about what a great guy Joe Hubbard was. Because he wasn't."

She smiled, this time. "Jealousy?"

Tom leaned back, stretching his shoulders. He rubbed his knee and felt its soreness. The ache was going, but the knee was tender to the touch. Some lassitude was coming to him. His voice was blurred. "What's in this drink?"

Her voice seemed far away. "A sedative. I thought you needed it. Sleep, lamb."

"No." He struggled to sit upright. "I—can't afford to—to sleep. I—"

She came over to help him to a full reclining position. Her voice was soft and soothing. "You can't afford not to, baby. You'll need your strength when it's time to run again."

The fragrance of her came to him and he felt the supple strength of her long fingers massaging the tight muscles of his shoulders. The taut face looked strangely maternal; he seemed to be drowning in the warm, brown eyes.

Just before he fell asleep he wondered which was the true girl; those soft eyes, or the rest of her?

He slept lightly, and dreamed. He dreamed of Joe and Lois together and Joe and Connie and Joe and Jean. Joe remained constant, but the girl kept changing like the colored lights in a juke box. He was no more than half asleep; the dream was as much daydream as night dream. Joe was the melody, riding the bass.

Joe had obviously been quite a stud, but that was only one of the immoralities. A friend's wife was no different

65

from a professional girl to the true studs. And to judge it honestly, who was hurt by any of it? Unless a person lived by the intangibles, now old-fashioned and scorned by the realists.

And yet, hadn't it brought Joe to a greater immorality? Wasn't it logical to think that he had thrown his friend to the wolves because of it? What had Jean said? *One corruption is all corruption.*

No. A white lie for social reasons is a long way this side of murder. And marital relations between unmarried adults could be a corruption only in the minds of the religious hysterics.

Or was that just something he wanted to believe?

And how about Miss Jean Revolt, the incorruptible? She'd gone to bed with him quickly enough. With no apparent moral compunctions. Let her practice what she preached.

He thought of Lois and their honeymoon and one particular night when they had achieved ideal communion. He remembered how she trembled and the strange things she'd said.

She'd said, "When you've lost communication with your God, you keep seeking it in people, don't you? And this seems to be the truest communication with people."

Was it?

Communication it certainly was. But the truest? At the time he'd chided her for voicing what he then considered sacrilege. Lois had always believed what she wanted to believe; she could rationalize black into white. Lois would be no oracle on the moralities.

Dogs didn't consider it communication; they didn't need to rationalize. Nor did dogs pull down any shades. But of course, neither did dogs write poetry or build bridges or donate blood to the Red Cross or . . .

Where the hell was he going?

He opened his eyes and saw Connie still sitting in the big chair. She was reading a book. Outside, he could hear a steady stream of traffic and he guessed that the boys from Douglas were coming home from work. Douglas finished the day shift a little after four; he couldn't have been sleeping long.

66

Tom asked, "What are you reading?"

She looked up and smiled. "Jack Woodford. Who else? This guy I can dig."

"What did you give me, goof-balls?"

She shook her head. "Not quite. Euphased. It's a partial sedative and a partial—well, do you know what euphoria is?"

Tom shook his head.

"Well, it means a sense of well-being, of buoyancy. That's what euphased gives you."

"Not me. I'm punchy. My lips tingle."

"Sleep, lamb. It must be that damned traffic. All the working stiffs are hurrying home so they won't miss Roy Rogers."

"I'd trade with any one of them." He slid up to prop his head on the cushioned end of the davenport. "I can't sleep. How the hell can I sleep with the law searching the town for me?"

She rose, and stretched. "They won't be bothering this end of town. There aren't enough cops for that. Could you eat? I could."

"I suppose. Damn it, though, I should do something. If I'm not going to stay here and work, I should get ready to run, again. I'd feel a hell of a lot safer out of the country."

"Patience. We want to be careful. You'll be ready to run in a day or so, but not until you've got a decent chance to get away clean. Pork chops all right?"

"My favorite fruit. I feel like a pimp."

"Easy, lamb. Think of what that would make me." She grimaced and went into the kitchen.

She came back in a minute with a copy of the *Daily News*. "Here, make like a husband, while I fuss over a hot frying pan."

There was nothing in the paper about Tom Spears. The flight from Jud Shallock's might have been caused by a routine check, but the man who'd come to Jean's had come prepared with a warrant. The fact that nothing about either visit was in the paper told Tom the police were sitting on this; they didn't want to scare him out of town. They wanted him here. And Jean wanted him here.

Connie, the realist, shared his earlier view. Connie had been living on the same side of the fence as he had; her faith in what the authorities called justice had been dulled by the facts.

He looked out the window behind him and saw the constant flow of traffic along the narrow street. A large percentage of the cars were jalopies; these were the "B" assemblers, who lived in Venice. In front of the restaurant across the street, a heavy man lounged, chewing on a toothpick.

Cop? The cop look.

Tom called, "Connie, if you're not tied up, I'd like you to inspect a man for me."

There was the slam of the refrigerator door and then Connie came into the room, wonder on her face. "Now what?"

Tom indicated the window. "Loafing in front of the restaurant. He looks like a cop, sort of."

The blonde studied him a moment and then shook her head. "I've seen him there before. If he's a cop, this is his beat. I think he could be a new resident. I never noticed him until a week ago."

Tom stared at her. "*Over* a week ago, I made my break."

Her voice was quiet and warm. "Tom, you're seeing ghosts. Stop it. *Nobody* knows about me and Joe, except you. We were never together except here. Joe was too big a man to be seen with Connie Garrity around town. I was surprised when he brought you here that night. Even drunk, Joe kept everything in its proper place."

His attention left the window and centered on her suddenly bleak face. "And you're still burning incense to the bastard's memory."

"He was a lot of man." She straightened. "I don't want to burn the pork chops." She went out stiffly.

Back street girl, accepting the inevitable. Riding with the tide and mingling with the masses. What was called the *easy* way, a drifter in the back eddies, selling what she must and withholding what she could. And never whimpering. Audibly.

From the kitchen, she called, "Dinner's ready."

He glanced out once more at the restaurant across the narrow street. But the man was gone.

In the kitchen, she was already seated, and the bleakness was gone from her face, the stiffness from her posture.

As he sat across from her, Tom said, "As a kid I was always good at one game. 'Run, sheep, run'; remember it?"

"Very well, lamb. I was kind of a flash at it, myself." She held out a platter of chops. "Except, of course, when I *wanted* to get caught."

He smiled. "Jean told me she used to run a lot, too. Her papa wasn't always wealthy, you know."

"Mmmm-hmmm. I know all about her. What line are we on, now?"

"I was thinking that maybe you envied her. Because she stopped running."

The brown eyes regarded him impersonally. "Were you, really? For your information, I *don't* envy her. I don't even feel for her enough to pity her. Would you like to talk about the weather?"

"I'd rather talk about you."

"All right, Mr. Spears, this is my routine." She was helping herself to the potatoes. "I work in a rather dimly lighted place. If you have a flashlight, you might be able to read the headline on a Hearst newspaper, that dim. In that kind of light, I look pretty good."

"You look pretty good, anyway."

"No interruptions, please. If we have a real, woolly lamb who thinks I might be available, I suggest that I might, too, but the hell of it is, the bartender would beef if I left early. However, if we should buy a bottle of champagne to take along, the bartender would not beef too much. More potatoes?"

Tom shook his head. "No, thanks."

"The champagne is not a good vintage, you understand, so it only costs between fifteen and twenty-five dollars a bottle, depending on how flush the lush looks. We are about to depart with it, when I suggest we open it and have one cozy drink between the three of us, for auld lang syne. Cute?"

Tom nodded, smiling. "And then you leave?"

"After one drink? No, I suggest another, and the bottle seems to disappear, and the lamb suggests we take off, but where is the bottle we are going to take along to my place? We must have another."

"But finally you *do* leave with the sucker?"

"Who can tell? He is getting drunk; if in the bartender's judgment, he is being unruly, he might get the old heave ho."

"You can't get much repeat business that way."

"Enough to make me wonder about them. Some people love to be abused; I think there's a name for the type."

"I know what you mean. But isn't there ever a time when ——" Tom paused, shrugging.

"There is occasionally a time, yes. If he is an exceptionally woolly lamb. I can't keep my hands off the really woolly ones."

"Even after you met Joe?"

"I didn't have anything left for the lambs after I met Joe."

From the street below came the wail of a siren, and Tom stiffened in his chair. Then, it wailed again, farther up the street.

Connie said softly, "If sirens bother you, you're in the wrong neighborhood, Tom. Most of them are ambulances, down here."

He relaxed in his chair.

Connie said, "Speaking of ambulances, how about that knee?"

"It's sore, but a lot better. It's going to be all right, I think."

"It's got to be, before you leave here. You may have to move fast on the road."

"If I run, yes." He rose to get the coffeepot from the stove.

When he turned around, again, he found her staring at him. "*If you run?* When did you get this change of heart?"

"I'm not sure I have. But I'm also not sure that running solves a damned thing."

"It might solve the problem of your continued existence. Or isn't that important? Maybe that euphased hasn't worn off."

"It's worn off. Connie, I want to be free. Women want security, I know, but all men want is to be free."

"In the clink, you'd be free?"

"I didn't kill my wife. If I can prove that, I'll be free again."

"Gawd," she said, "And you a former bookie." She held

70

up her cup to be filled. She shook her head and looked sadly past him.

He filled his own cup and put the pot back on the stove. "I won't stay here, of course. That would be criminal. I'll get in touch with what few solvent friends I can trust and find a place to operate from. Jean might have some angles, by now. She was getting some—material this afternoon. I'll get in touch with her."

"Not tonight, you won't. They probably have her phone tapped, right now."

"All right, not tonight. But some way, tomorrow."

"We'll talk about it tomorrow."

"If you have a car," Tom suggested, "I could go to a booth in another section of town and phone some people. I wouldn't want the call traced back to here."

"Not tonight, Tom. We'll watch television and get drunk." She smiled. "Not too drunk, though, huh? I don't want you to have any excuses, in case you should get ideas."

Chapter 6

HE DIDN'T get any ideas. Maybe it was the drug she'd given him or maybe it was the soreness of his knee or maybe it was because he'd made his decision Jean's way. At any rate, they sat and watched TV, a western movie involving some men in light hats and some men in black hats and a chase and a fine fight and ricocheting bullets, and then a chase started, again—and Tom fell asleep on the davenport.

When he wakened, the room was dark and his shoes were off and there was a blanket over him and a pillow under his head. The lustful Florence Nightingale, the collector of lost lambs, the Grade-A "B" girl . . .

If Joe hadn't been drunk that night and he hadn't been with him, he never would have known about her at all. Joe hadn't ever been a real drinking man; it was an unusual combination of incidents that had revealed Connie to Joe. There were probably other incidents in Joe's life that had been buried with him.

And some that might not have been. Jean could know, by now.

In the narrow street below, a hot rod's bark disturbed the quiet night air. Tom raised himself to a sitting position and looked out. There was a dim light in the restaurant across the street, a night light. No other light showed in the neighborhood.

Tom swung his legs to the floor and felt his injured knee. Some of the swelling had gone down but the knee was still tender. He fumbled on the coffee table nearby until he found his cigarettes and groped some more until he found the table lighter he knew was there.

The flare of the lighter and then the glow of his cigarette and an apprehension in him stronger than when he'd gone to sleep. The dark, probably; he had never liked the dark.

This was the darkest dark, immediately before dawn; he hadn't finished his cigarette when the first gray streaks of it appeared in the sky over the restaurant.

In the houses all around him, the workers would be stirring, getting ready for their day of toil. Tom had never learned much about honest labor; it was another of the things he had run from. There had always been so many easier ways to make a dollar.

The image of Jean Revolt was vivid in his mind. He tried to analyze her attraction for him, the lure of her which certainly extended beyond the bed.

In her room at the end of the hall, Connie would be sleeping, and he wondered if he'd been a disappointment to her. He had slept with worse. He had been married to worse.

That wasn't fair, that last thought; that had been a spiteful, cheap thought about a woman who had given him infinite ecstasy. And she was now dead. Murdered.

By whom?

Joe Hubbard? Maybe. If so, who'd murdered Joe?

Jean wanted to know that and Jean would work on it until she learned who had or until she ran into the final blind alley. Her father's daughter, Jean Revolt.

But vulnerable, like all the bleeding hearts. Vulnerable to a wolf like Joe Hubbard and a lamb like Tom Spears.

It was almost light in the room, now. Tom rose and went

72

into the kitchen. He filled the coffeepot with water and took the oleo out of the refrigerator.

He warmed some milk and drank it. He turned the flame lower under the coffeepot and went into the bathroom to shave. Connie had a razor in there, and some new blades.

Through the small, bathroom window he could see the flat, grayish water of the Pacific. Gulls walked the littered sand; one hardy early-morning-dipper moved through the placid water in a steady eight beat crawl.

He was measuring the coffee into the top of the percolator when Connie came into the kitchen. She wore a robe over her night gown; her bleached hair was tied high on her head with a ribbon.

"I used your razor," Tom said.

"Well, that's an affectionate greeting. Why the early bird routine?"

"I couldn't sleep. The nap, I suppose—" He smiled at her. "You'll be rid of me today."

"I'm in no hurry." She came over to put a hand on his shoulder. "Do you know what you're doing, Tom?"

He watched the water start to percolate and set the timer. "No, Connie. I only know what I *have* to do."

She sighed. "Men. Men can never ride with the tide, can they? They always have to stir up trouble."

He turned to face her. "Do you really think I should run? You don't think running would be wrong, cowardly?"

"I'm no girl to judge between right and wrong, honey. I guess you'll have to do what you have to do. I don't want to talk about it."

"But—"

She gestured wearily. "But me no buts. How is that knee?"

"Much better. I'll get around."

"All right. How do you want your eggs?"

"Connie, listen, please." He put his hands on her shoulders and looked down at her earnestly. "I want you to understand this. You've offered me a refuge and have a right to know if I'm going to risk revealing your part in this. I never will. There aren't enough cops in this town to worm your name out of me. Is that what you're worried about?"

She shook her head. "Not even slightly. What bothers me

73

is knowing you're falling for the Revolt girl's line. But that's another thing I'm through talking about. Tom, our brief and happy relationship is ended when you walk out of here. No words, please, and no tears."

She twisted out of his grasp and went over to the refrigerator. She took out a bottle of orange juice and a carton of eggs. Tom went over to sit in the upholstered nook near the door.

Below, he could see the restaurant. And the '51 Chev Club parked in front of it. And the man behind the wheel. The man seemed to be waiting for someone, slouched in the seat, smoking a cigarette.

Tom said, "I think our lounger is back. On wheels, this time. A Chev Club, parked in front of the restaurant."

She was cracking eggs into a bowl. "Maybe he's waiting for the restaurant to open." She cracked the last of the eggs and came over to the window. "Same man? Are you sure?"

"Fairly sure. Wish I had some binoculars."

"I've some opera glasses, believe it or not. Wait." She went out.

The man in the Chev didn't look up; his gaze was straight ahead through the windshield. The restaurant was closed; Connie's guess could make sense.

When she came back, she handed him a pair of mother-of-pearl opera glasses and he focused them on the man across the street.

It wasn't a face Tom recognized nor a face that would be remembered if seen infrequently. It was broad and placid and not distinguished by any unusual features, a John Doe sort of face.

Connie said, "Let me see him. I recognized the other man and if this is the same one, we shouldn't worry."

In a few moments, she lowered the glasses. "Same man. A nothing. He surely doesn't look like any kind of menace." She put the glasses on the table and went back to beat the eggs.

Tom had seen killers who looked less dangerous, torpedos who wouldn't look out of place at the Union League Club. He sipped his orange juice and said nothing.

A few minutes later, a man came to open the restaurant

and a few minutes after that, the occupant of the Chev went in.

"Maybe you were right," Tom told Connie. "He just went into the restaurant."

"We'll see." She started to say more, and stopped.

Tom smiled. "Say it. Whatever it is, I can take it."

"Just this—be careful, won't you? Be careful every second." She took a breath. "And if you find Miss Revolt dull, I'm always home days."

"Miss Revolt," Tom told her, "is carrying the torch, still, same as you are, for a man I don't want to talk about."

"Maybe. Your appeal is different, Tom, but just as strong. And you're no fighter. Don't let anybody talk you into a corner."

"I promise."

Half an hour later, when they had finished the dishes, the Chev Club was still parked across the street.

"Maybe he works there," Connie suggested. "Maybe he was finishing his day, yesterday, when we saw him."

"Maybe. But I don't want to go out where he can see me. I've a feeling about him."

Connie went to the window, to stare out at the car. "I could go past the place; I need to go to the store. If I see him working in there, we'll know he's all right. If he's just sitting—" She turned to face Tom. "Well, if he's just sitting—what next?"

"If he's just sitting, I'll have to leave here without his seeing me. Can that be done?"

She nodded. "The stairs aren't in sight of that restaurant. And you could walk right to the beach, and down a few blocks and I'd pick you up down there." She paused. "But not now. The least I can do is get you readier than you are, first."

Tom frowned. "The knee—you mean?"

"The face, I mean. I know where I can get a fine mustache and I have a pair of spectacles, here, horn-rimmed jobs that—"

"No," Tom interrupted. "The glasses make sense, but no mustache. I'd feel so damned self-conscious, I'd automatically make people suspicious."

She studied him a few moments. "All right. I'm through arguing. I'll get dressed and take my stroll. You keep an eye on me through the window. Once the man sees me leave, he may try to come up here." She went out.

When she came through, again, dressed, all the warmth was gone from her face. She put a spectacle case on the table in front of Tom and went out the door without a word.

Tom opened the case and looked at the horn-rimmed glasses within. He tried them on, and there was no distortion of vision. Theatrical glasses with flat lenses.

He saw her come around the corner of the building below and head directly across the street. But she didn't walk *past* the restaurant.

She went in.

A quick apprehension moved through him. But almost as quickly, he realized it was the best way to check on the man. If she had stayed on this side of the street, it was possible she couldn't see into the restaurant. If she crossed here, it would seem illogical, inasmuch as the corner was only a few buildings down the street. She could go in and order a cup of coffee without being suspect.

He sat and waited and the apprehension came back. He didn't take his eyes from the restaurant door as the seconds dragged by. It would not be her natural instinct to walk boldly into trouble; this thing she was doing for him ran counter to the trend of her living, of drifting with the tide.

He told himself she would need to spend some time in the place. The more leisurely she was, dawdling over coffee and a cigarette, the less suspicious she would be. Unless the man was watching this place. In which case, her entry would strengthen his belief.

The door opened, and she came out and Tom breathed easier. She didn't head for the market, however. She came straight across the street again and disappeared around the corner of the building.

He heard her feet on the wooden stairs outside and was facing the door when she opened it.

Her eyes met his without apparent interest. "He's just sitting in there, at a table, facing the window."

"Did he say anything to you?"

She shook her head. "I know the proprietor, there. I told him I was out of coffee and had to drink his bilge, this morning. Very light, very casual. I was scared, but I don't think my voice showed it."

"If the man is watching for me," Tom said, "he'd be in a place where he could watch that door."

"Where the sun is, now, he can see the door and the steps. They're reflected in that bay window across the court."

"Did he look like a cop?"

"Not the kind I've met."

"I'll go," Tom said, after a few seconds. "If there's any other way out, I'll take it. He's no cop. He'd have been here with a warrant, if he was a cop. He must be somebody who thinks I know something." Tom paused. "And maybe he thinks you know something, too, now, Connie."

Her voice was dead. "Maybe. There is a back way out, over the roof of the garage. You could walk down to the beach from there, and I'd wait the block this side of Windward. It's a '48 Ford Tudor, deep blue."

Tom shook his head. "You've done too much already. I'll get away all right."

"No. I want you as safe as possible. You owe that to me. I don't want you caught, for my own protection."

His voice was gentle. "You're doing this for me, because you want to help a man in trouble. Why don't you admit that, at least to yourself?"

"Maybe I do—to myself. Try the glasses. I want to see how you look."

Tom put them on, and she studied him a few seconds. Then she nodded. "Gives you a scholarly look, entirely different. Come on; I'll show you the way out."

"First I should know where I'm going." Tom said. He rose and got the phone book.

The office of Leonard Delavan was on Selma in Hollywood. Tom closed the book, again, and said, "I'll take the red bus from here."

From here to Beverly Hills and the streetcar from Beverly Hills to Hollywood. This part of it he didn't voice.

"I'll take you further away than the bus stop," she told

him. "I don't want to know where you're going." She looked past him. "If they put the pressure on me, I won't have the guts to shut up about this. So, for your own protection, I don't want to know where you're going."

"I'm going to Beverly Hills, first." He put the spectacle case into his pocket. "To look over my property. If the police should ask."

"Police?" Her smile was bleak. "That's the least of our troubles, isn't it?"

He stared. "But you said 'they.' You said 'they' might put the pressure on you. Didn't you mean the police?"

"If that man in the restaurant is a policeman, I meant the police."

He came over to stand in front of her and grip her shoulders once more. "Connie, if you know something, tell me. That's the best way, all around."

She looked at him, and away. "If I *knew* anything, you'd have had it yesterday. Not today, but yesterday. I know you were mixed up with gamblers and with Joe Hubbard. What other kind of yeggs you two knew, I don't know. But there must have been some killers in the bunch."

"Gamblers, the kind I worked with and for, aren't killers, Connie. Con men and honest gamblers *never* kill. That's SOP."

"All right. ALL RIGHT!" She twisted from his grasp. "I don't want to play detective. I'll show you the window that leads to the top of the garage next door. It's not much of a drop from the garage."

He didn't argue further. He followed her to her bedroom and she showed him how he would have to stretch to cover the few feet from the window to the flat roof of the garage. From the western end of the roof, he could drop into a vacant lot.

"You can follow the beach from there to Windward," she said. "I'll pick you up there, or a block this side of it, wherever I can park."

"Okay." He looked at her, trying to find some words, but none came.

She stayed behind until he was dressed and out on the flat roof. Then she closed the window and locked it.

78

He came to the far end of the roof and looked down. There would be a drop of only a few feet, if he hung from this edge. He looked around, but nobody was watching him. The alley ran along the front of the garage; below him was a sandy, weed-filled lot.

The knee was still sore, but if he hung full length, there would be very little drop. He kept the right leg slightly bent, took the shock of the fall along the left side of his body. He kept the garage between him and the restaurant as he walked down toward the beach.

Where Seventeenth dead-ended, he turned back toward Speedway. The '48 Ford was waiting no more than twenty feet from the corner. She opened the door on the curb side as she saw him approach. The motor was running.

Tom climbed in and closed the door, and the Ford was moving with the click of the latch. Connie said, "As far as I know, the creep's still sitting in the restaurant. But I'll make a few turns, just to be on the safe side."

On Windward, she turned right, but continued past Main, which was the through artery to Santa Monica. A block down, she cut off this new street and started zigzagging back toward Main.

Tom, who'd been watching the rear, said, "Not a Chevrolet in sight. I hope he doesn't bother you, Connie."

"You don't hope it as much as I do." They were back on Main, now, heading for Santa Monica. "Outside of the police, nobody bothers me too much."

"We could be wrong about him," Tom said. "It doesn't figure that anyone would know there was a possibility of my going to your place. Only four people knew about that time Joe brought me there. Unless that girl who went to Milwaukee—"

Connie shook her head. "No. Not her. Maybe you were followed from Jean's place."

"Maybe. But I'd bet a hundred to one against it."

"Well, then, maybe we were seeing ghosts. But don't worry about me, Tom. I'll get by. Would you light me a cigarette?"

He lighted her a cigarette and handed it to her. She offered no further conversation all the way to Beverly Hills.

There, near the post office, Tom said, "This will be fine.

79

I'll keep in touch with you, Connie, after I'm clear, again."

Her smile was bleak. "Mmmm-hmmm. Luck, lamb. God knows you'll need it."

"Do you think I'm being foolish, Connie?"

"I've stopped thinking. Hurry; we don't want to get pinched for double parking."

He opened the door. "Thank you for everything. I'll never forget it."

He was outside, the door handle still in his grasp, when she put the car in motion again. He slammed the door hurriedly and stepped back as the rear tires squealed under the rush of power. The Ford shot up the street and Connie didn't look back.

Women . . .

He was now in Beverly Hills, the most vigorously policed area in America, and his former home. Someone could recognize him; he hurried to the car line.

It was a clanking, tedious ride to Hollywood. Tom sat near the rear, where he could watch anyone who entered. The car held about a dozen passengers, none of whom showed any interest in him.

The office building on Selma was a five story, stucco monstrosity in pseudo-Spanish architecture, a maze of halls and stairs and turns. The office of Leonard Delavan—*Investigations* was on the second floor, across from a reading fee literary agency.

Tom was in luck; Delavan had the door to the waiting room open and Tom could see through into the inner office where Delavan sat at his desk.

But he couldn't see if anyone else was in the office; he waited in the open doorway to the hall.

In a few moments, Delavan looked up. He rose immediately, gesturing Tom in.

Tom came in as Delavan entered the waiting room. The detective locked the hall door and took a deep breath of relief. "We've been worried about you. Come into the office."

Tom came in, and Delavan closed that door, too. Tom sat in an upholstered chair on the customer's side of the big desk; Delavan went back to his former seat.

The detective shook his head. "That was no policeman,

the man who sent you running from Jean's place. We found that out, later. He had the badge and a warrant, but they were both phony."

"Phony? But the siren?"

Delavan shrugged. "Maybe he had one, or it might have been a lucky coincidence for him. Maybe an ambulance was going by as he turned off Channel."

"But he was looking for me. Who else could it be but the law, if he was looking for me?"

"The killer, maybe?" Delavan's eyes were steady on Tom's. "Or an agent of the killer's? Your guess would be as good as mine." He picked up a letter opener on his desk, and studied it. "You know, Tom, we weren't too sure of you, at first. The night Jean dropped you off at Jud Shallock's, I kept an eye on the place. We guessed you were innocent, but we weren't sure. I'm sure, now."

"Thank you," Tom said dryly. "I suppose that's a help."

"It could be. Where have you been?"

"At a friend's house. I think I was being watched, there, too." He went on to explain about the man in the Chev coupe. He didn't reveal the address, however, nor the identity of Connie.

When he'd finished, Delavan said, "How sure are you of this friend who sheltered you? You wouldn't want to give me his name?"

"No. He doesn't know I came here, either."

Delavan had the point of the letter opener on the blotter top of his desk and he was flexing the blade. He kept his gaze on that. "An old friend, was he? Tied up in the gambling business?"

"No. A friend I met only once before. And not tied up in gambling. Why? What has that to do with it?"

"Because I don't think we can trust your old friends." Delavan put the letter opener carefully down on the desk and looked up at Tom. "Who is our most logical suspect as a killer of both your wife and Joe Hubbard?"

Tom thought for only a moment and then said, "Jean Revolt."

Delavan frowned. "Are you trying to be humorous?"

"You asked for an opinion," Tom said. "If she's a jealous

type and had learned Joe and Lois were—well, doesn't it figure?"

"Not to me." Delavan's eyes were hard.

"Nor me," Tom agreed. "Because I know her, now. But to a cop who knew what we know?"

"I'm sure," Delavan said slowly, "she's alibied for the times of both murders. Guess again, Tom, with more sense."

"I haven't any other guess with as much sense."

"Well, then, here's a hint for you. We learned yesterday, from Joe's records, that Nannie Koronas paid for that farce of a legal defense Joe butchered you with."

"That figures. Nannie takes care of his own. That's why he's got the employee loyalty he has."

"Yes? And how well he took care of you, sending you away for life. Is that taking care of his employees?"

"He hired a good lawyer. The lawyer botched it, maybe. But the lawyer died, too, after botching it, didn't he? Now *that* kill could have been financed by Nannie. Except for one thing." Tom paused. "Nannie doesn't work that way. Nannie does very well, playing the track percentage with limits. He doesn't have to go heavy."

"I know. None of them have to, but they all do, eventually. And this—did Joe Hubbard ever tell you Koronas was paying for the defense?"

"No—no, he didn't." Tom was suddenly thoughtful.

"I wonder why?" Delavan said icily. "Maybe because he sent Joe there to lose that case. And maybe Joe knew why and tried a little blackmail later—and got his. That makes more sense than anything else we've come across, Tom. And that might be why they're after you, now."

"But why would Nannie want me out of the way? I made money for him, never cheated him out of a nickel. It simply doesn't add."

"Maybe he thinks you know something. Maybe he thinks you got to St. Louis earlier than you did and learned something. Or you know who your wife was going to meet in St. Louis."

"Oh, that's reaching," Tom said. "Lois hardly knew Nannie; she'd only met him a couple of times."

"To your knowledge."

Silence, while the three words went around in Tom's mind. Across the desk from him, Delavan's face blurred for a second in Tom's vision.

Delavan's voice was gentle. "A nasty thing to surmise, maybe, but we've learned nastier about her, already, haven't we?"

"If it's true," Tom said, "we're lost. We haven't got a chance against Nannie Koronas."

"Maybe we have. Joe did other jobs for him. We learned that, yesterday, too. Though there's nothing incriminating in any of it, so far."

"There won't be. Nannie's smart. He's always covered."

Delavan nodded slowly. "I know, I know. But he's worried about you, isn't he? He's got his boys out searching the town for you."

"We don't know. That man in the restaurant could be no more than a man in a restaurant. We don't *know* anything."

"No," Delavan admitted wearily, "we don't." He stood up. "I've got to find a place for you. Our only hope is to keep you free and staked out." He smiled. "Like a sacrificial lamb."

Chapter 7

THE APARTMENT building was an eight unit, two-story, weathered, rectangular stucco place on Kenmore. They went down the narrow, first-floor hall to the apartment on the right in the rear, and Delavan unlocked the door.

It was a furnished place of living room, sleeping alcove, kitchen and bath, bright and not too sadly furnished.

"How about the landlord?" Tom asked.

"I'm the landlord. Nothing like a few rental properties to keep the income constant. I'm not in a stable trade, you know." He handed Tom the key. "I'll go out and pick you up some groceries."

In the quiet apartment, Tom sat on a cushioned rattan davenport and lighted a cigarette. There was some throb in his knee, again; there was perspiration dampening the back of his collar.

How long could he do nothing, a puppet in the hands of the more determined? None of them knew as much about the Koronas organization as he did. If the secret of Joe's death, of Lois' death was buried in the mind of Nannie Koronas, they were working in vain. But if others in the organization had been involved?

Jud Shallock? Jud knew about Lois; Jud had presumed Tom had found Lois with somebody and killed her. And yet, Jud hadn't known Lois well to Tom's knowledge. And yet, he knew *about* Lois.

Everybody in town, it seemed, knew about Lois. Except her husband. Which appeared to be the standard situation in that kind of case.

He rose, after a few minutes, and went from window to window, like a gopher making sure of its emergency exits. There was a rear door, leading off the kitchen into the fenced back yard. The incinerator was out there and the clotheslines and a gate in the high redwood fence that evidently opened on an alley.

He came back to the rattan davenport and was sitting there when Delavan opened the door. The investigator said, "I've a master key, so there'll *never* be any reason for you to answer the doorbell. Anyone who rings or knocks doesn't belong out there."

Tom nodded.

Delavan took the bag of groceries he was carrying out to the kitchen, and came back to the living room. "You look beat, Tom."

"I am. I'm licked, but good. I'm sick of it."

Delavan sat in a rattan chair and fished for a cigarette. "I suppose. Feel kind of hopeless, don't you?"

"Worse. I feel like a pimp. Is Miss Revolt's money financing all this?"

"Mmmm-hmmm." Delavan lighted his cigarette. "If we prove you innocent, you can pay her back. With interest."

"How? In old *Racing Forms?*"

"In cash. If you're innocent, your late wife's money will be yours, Tom. You'll be rich."

"Migawd, I will be. That's right. I never thought of that. Not that I want it."

"She had no other relatives. Do you think the state needs it worse than you do? Get smart. The state has made a lot more off of horse racing than you ever did. Do you want them to have *this*, too?"

Tom managed a smile. "Well, that's the right approach. No, I don't. Okay, Hawkshaw, I'll sit tight for a few more hours."

Delavan frowned. "And then——? And then, you'll start running again?"

Tom shook his head slowly. "No, then I'll start working, personally. So I'll feel like a man."

Delavan rose. "You can't do it. It could jeopardize all our work. With a little more knowledge, we can go to the Governor and make a case against extraditing you. Right now, you'd be a dead duck if they got you back to Missouri."

"Okay. Okay." Tom rose, too. "How will I keep in touch? I suppose the phone's been disconnected in here?"

"It has. I'll keep in touch with you. Don't get restless or reckless, Tom. Trust us." He paused. "Remember one thing: so long as Nannie doesn't find you, he'll be wondering what you know. It will bother him, if he's as guilty as we think he is. It's the only way we can get him to show his hand, to keep him scared."

"Okay. Okay. You don't know the man, but okay."

For a moment, Delavan looked as weary as Tom felt. "I know the man. Stay quiet. Try and relax." He gestured and went to the door. A moment he stood there, listening, and then he went out without looking back.

Try and relax . . . Yes. He wished Connie had given him some of that euphased to take along. He wondered about her, if that big, bland nothing in the Chev coupe had finally climbed the wooden steps to her apartment.

Some world he'd occupied, a world in which he'd seen only the surface, a world of mass infidelity and brutal undercurrents. Perhaps, though, it was his fault; he hadn't been interested enough to search beneath the surface. Working for Nannie hadn't seemed particularly immoral. Illegal it certainly was, but what was immoral about banking against those who speculated on the speed of horses?

It was outside the law, and the representatives of the

people made the law. And once a man was outside it, however slightly, it was easier to go outside the moral code on which laws should be based.

To his knowledge, Nannie was involved in nothing but gambling. But perhaps that was another area where he hadn't gone beneath the surface. There'd been no reason to; he had his four bills a week and very little trouble from the law. He'd dealt with suckers who considered it ungentlemanly to beef too much over a loss and who would never be guilty of informing the police.

A fine life with a rich and eager wife; only a fool would have speculated on the worth of it or dug into the patina of it, searching for trouble.

Nobody wanted trouble. Except for the reformers, the blue-noses, the agitators, the Commies. They lived on trouble, thrived on it, came to power on it. All the John Does wanted was a roof and a full larder and a few bucks to blow now and then.

And yet, it was the agitators who finally got the John Does to a point where the larder was full and the roof their own. The right wing agitators like Henry Ford and the left wing agitators like John L. Lewis. Neither of these gentlemen could be called conformist, each in his way was a radical. Each had contributed.

And now the daughter of one of America's great mavericks was sticking her neck out for a drifter named Tom Spears. And he had doubted her motives, even while he accepted her sanctuary.

He closed his eyes and saw the short, dark hair, the direct gaze of the deep blue eyes, the slim, active figure. Spending her money, risking her freedom. For what?

To find the killer of a man she now knew as a fraud? To nail the biggest operator of a racket she despised? To save the neck of a man she had met only once?

It was something more intangible than that, and she'd voiced it for him. She'd said, "I can't fight all the injustice in the world. But I intend to fight all the injustice that touches me."

She'd be overmatched against Nannie Koronas, though.

Even with an ally as capable as Leonard Delavan.

In the bathroom mirror, Tom studied his face. He had lost weight, in prison, and his face was thinner. This made his head appear longer and narrower; the horn-rimmed glasses added the final touch. He did, as Connie had said, look scholarly now. People who had known him only casually might not recognize him. No person who had seen his picture in the papers nor a policeman who'd seen it on fliers would be likely to recognize him.

Delavan had warned him against getting "restless or reckless." But he was restless. And was it recklessness to try and save his neck? He wasn't accustomed to having others fight his battles for him.

Who did he know in the organization? He knew Jud well. He knew a score of minor bookies on the Jud Shallock level around town. And he knew Nannie's girl friend, a former burlesque stripper now trying for a foothold in Hollywood. A beautiful girl, really, and something of a social climber.

She'd shown a definite interest in Tom at a party one time at Nannie's. But Tom had guessed it was because of Lois' social prominence. And the girl had been more than half drunk.

But . . . ? There was an angle, however weak. That night, at Nannie's, he could have moved in; she'd made no bones about that. Tom's wasn't the degree of vanity that permitted him to think he was in any way irresistible to women. But he'd been luckier than most from the time he was fifteen; it would be false modesty to overlook his appeal in a search for weapons.

He'd need a bigger weapon, too, a weapon with a trigger, a weapon that went "bang." He'd be hunting a killer; his doubtful sex appeal would be a pitiful armament against that.

It was now early afternoon. He lay on the rattan davenport, scouring his memory, going back through the years to his first association with Nannie Koronas, trying to dredge up every rumor and fact he knew or had heard.

There was so damned little; it was a requisite of the security Nannie enjoyed that no member of the organization see the whole picture. The Kefauver Committee had hardly touched him; the reports had been so conflicting, the witnesses so obviously prepared with only half-truths and unprovable rumors.

Tom had known Nannie better than any of the other employees at the customer level. Tom had been married to Lois and Tom was friendly with a number of big money betters. Yet Tom knew very little about him, except that Nannie was extremely wealthy, apparently genial and undoubtedly attractive in his virile, predatory way.

His father had been a poverty-ridden Greek cobbler, his mother Scotch-Irish. His mother had died when Nannie was twelve and he had left home six months later. It was his boast that he had made his own way from that day on.

In the quiet furnished apartment on Kenmore, Tom remembered with what pride Nannie had looked back on his career. He liked to think of himself as a business executive, another living proof of the Horatio Alger legend.

It didn't seem logical, now, that Nannie would ever have gone in for murder. The futile dedication of inveterate horse players was a constant, depression-proof, cash market that afforded Nannie all the income a reasonable man could want.

Nannie paid track odds up to the limit of twenty-to-one. That was a percentage the track and the state could get rich on and Nannie's twenty-to-one limitation gave him that additional percentage. With the organization he had covering the field, he couldn't go broke. He had expenses, but certainly no more than the tracks had, and all the tracks prospered.

Why, then, murder?

It didn't add, it didn't figure.

Outside, in the hallway, there were steps on the bare floor and Tom sat up quickly on the davenport.

There was the sound of a key in the lock and then the door opened and Leonard Delavan came in. He closed the door quietly behind him.

"Trouble?" Tom asked. "You look worried."

"I am. What kind of car was that you told me about a little while ago, the one parked in front of where you were hiding?"

"A '51 Chev Club coupe."

"Sand gray?"

Tom nodded.

"What'd the driver look like?"

"Nothing special. Big, bland round face. A big piece of nothing."

Delavan took a deep breath. "Same man. He's parked in front of the entrance to my office building, right now. I parked in the parking lot, luckily, and spotted the car from the other side of the street. I didn't like the way he was sitting there and then I remembered what you'd told me about the Chev."

"It figures," Tom said, "that if they knew about Jean, they'd know about you."

Delavan shook his head. "Not to me, it doesn't figure. Jean was Joe's fiancée; she's logical enough to them. There was no secret about her relationship to Joe. But nobody knew about my working for her, nobody but Joe's attorney."

"And the man or men who watched you visit Joe's attorney and visit Jean."

"Oh, I was careful about that."

"Not careful enough, evidently. Leonard, have you an extra gun?"

Delavan stared at him for seconds, and then reached under his jacket to come up with a short-barreled .38. "You can have this one. I'll pick up another at the office when I can get back there."

Tom was silent a moment. Then, "I suppose you couldn't report the guy in the Chev to the police."

"Report him for what? Parking? And if I knew something about him, they'd want to know what kind of case I was on. No, I can't go to the law this time."

Tom paused again. "And—you don't want to face him?"

Delavan looked at the floor. "Two have died already. I've been a private investigator for a long time, but private investigators don't work on murder cases. I'm no hero. I'll come face to face with him eventually, I don't doubt. Maybe this is one of my—gutless afternoons."

"I wasn't criticizing," Tom said quietly. "I only wondered if he means to get rough. Maybe he just wants to buy his information."

"Maybe. The man who posed as a detective to Jean, yesterday, didn't answer the description of this man. So there must be more than one man looking for you." He lifted his head to meet Tom's gaze. "Try and forget what I said a few minutes ago. It isn't only that the man might be armed. It's also my precarious position in this case. If the police should learn I harbored a fugitive, all the years of my training would be wasted. *I'd be out of business.*"

Tom smiled at him. "Leonard, I don't need any lengthy explanations. You've stuck your neck out too far, already. And I appreciate it. And you'll never be involved through any words of mine."

Delavan walked over to the window and looked out into the side yard. He kept his back to Tom as he said, "That Jean gets a man all hopped up on the intangibles like justice and fighting evil and a million things a sensible man should realize is juvenile. It was different, working for her dad. He was a realist. And he was a businessman." Delavan turned, "And so am I."

"I know," Tom said. "But nobody's twisting your arm, Leonard."

"That's right. Nobody is. Okay; maybe the man in the Chev is gone, now. I'll get in touch with you. Stay here; that gun's for self-protection, only." He nodded and went out.

Naval Intelligence and the FBI . . . Well, maybe the man thought he'd earned a chance at the quieter life, the safe life of divorce cases and missing persons, of go-between and watching warehouses.

And, Tom reflected, it wasn't *Delavan's* life the man was working to save. That would make a big difference. It was *his* neck, and what was he doing? He was hiding, waiting, hoping.

He tried the .38 in his jacket pocket, but it sagged too much. He wedged it between the waistband of his trousers and his shirt and then buttoned his coat. He walked a few steps and the gun seemed secure enough.

He flexed the knee, which now had almost complete articulation, despite its tenderness. He was no hero; he stared at the door for seconds, a queasiness in his stomach, before turning the knob and going out into the hall.

There, again, he paused before walking along the narrow passage toward the bright, late afternoon showing through the glass of the front door.

From a drugstore on Sunset, he phoned Jud Shallock, but nobody answered. He turned back to the "P's" in the phone book and found Prentice, Lisa Prentice. He'd expected her to have an unlisted number; maybe she wasn't Nannie's favorite any more.

The address was on Sunset and not too far; he took a cab.

It was a luxury apartment, with a view of the city behind it, and a view of the hills to the front. In the carpeted lobby, Tom pressed the button next to Lisa Prentice's card.

Her voice sounding raspy through the speaker. "Ames——?"

"No," Tom said. "Is this Lisa?"

"Yes. Who is it?"

"A former employee of Nannie's. I don't want to come up if there's a chance——"

"Tom——? Tom Spears?"

"Right."

"Come on up. Nobody's here."

Two steps above him, the door buzzed and he went up and through it. The self-service elevator was here, its door open. He stepped in and pressed the button for the sixth floor.

Ames? she'd asked. Was it Ames Gilchrist she'd been expecting, the doorknob tryer, the one Jean had suspected of carrying pornographic postcards?

Lisa Prentice was standing in the doorway of her apartment when Tom got off the elevator. She was a small and exquisitely boned female with jet black hair and high coloring. Except for an overabundance of bust, her slight figure was beautifully proportioned. She was dressed in a candy-striped silk.

Her brown eyes considered him gravely as he walked along the carpeted hallway toward her. "This is some surprise," she said. "Remembered me, did you?"

"Nobody's likely to forget you, Lisa. Did you expect *me* to?" He paused a few feet from her, smiling down at her.

Her oval face held a tinge of mockery. "I see you didn't

91

lose any of your charm in prison. What honestly brought you here, Tom?"

He said nothing for seconds, holding her gaze. Then he said, "I thought you might know something that would help. I'll go, if you want, Lisa."

She shook her head, and stood to one side. "Come in, Tom."

He came into a small, circular entrance hall, through an archway from that into a living room with full length windows flanking an ebony, high-hearth fireplace. Through the windows he could see the city for miles.

Lisa gestured toward a ten foot, circular davenport upholstered in a nubby, lime-colored fabric. "Make yourself comfortable. Drink?"

Tom sat rigidly on the edge of the davenport. "Not now, thanks. You were expecting someone, were you?"

"Ames Gilchrist. Know him?" She was mixing herself a drink at a quilted, leatherette bar near the archway.

"Never heard of him," Tom lied. "A friend of Nannie's, is he?"

She turned from the bar, a drink in her hand. "Why should he be?"

"I only asked. I hoped he wasn't. I've a feeling Nannie might be a man to stay away from. Am I right?"

Her gaze dropped to the drink in her hand and then back to meet Tom's. "He could be." She came over to sit some distance away on the davenport. "Yes, he very well could be. He—was out of town the night your wife was killed."

A few seconds and then Tom said, "Which proves nothing, of course. Nannie goes out of town quite often."

"Not too often. He hired Joe Hubbard, too, to defend you. Joe was a friend of yours, wasn't he?"

Tom nodded.

Lisa sipped her drink. "*Some friend!* Though he did save you from the gas chamber, didn't he?"

Tom said nothing.

Lisa tried to sound casual, and missed it. "Where have you been hiding, Tom?"

He looked at her blankly. "A—hotel in a bad part of town.
92

Lisa, do you think Nannie killed my wife?"

"I don't know. He was sleeping with her, I know, and he was out of town the time she was killed." She pulled her legs up under her. "You were true to your wife, weren't you, Tom?"

"I was. I guess I was a sucker. Aren't you and Nannie still —well—"

"He still likes me, yes. I can't be sure I'm first in his affections any more, but we're still friends. Why, Tom?"

"Because the way you accused him, well—it doesn't add, if you're his girl."

"I'm not his girl. I'm nobody's girl, and especially a has-been like Nannie. The Eastern boys are taking him over, Tom. He's fighting, but—" She shrugged.

"They've tried it before. Nannie's Mr. Big in this end of the state. He's run the Eastern trash out before."

"He's bought them off, before. These new boys don't buy."

"Who are they?"

She shrugged. "All I know is how he's whining about the competition. I'm sick of listening to it." She finished her drink. "Can't I mix you a little something? You look like you could use it."

"All right. Bourbon and water will do it."

She was mixing it when the phone rang. She picked up the instrument and said, "Hello." A pause and then, "I'll manage to keep busy. Phone before you come over. I might go to a show with one of the girls." A chuckle. "One of the *girls*, I said. Bye."

She replaced the phone and said to Tom, "That was Ames. He won't be over." She was smiling as she turned back to mix the drinks.

It was the kind of smile a strip-teaser learns early and probably meant nothing, Tom thought.

When she came back with the drinks, she said, "If you should clear your name, you'd be rich, wouldn't you, Tom? Your wife's money would be yours."

"I guess it would."

She chuckled. "You'd be quite a prize." She went back

to her former seat. "Any girl would consider you a good catch." She wasn't looking at him. "*Any* girl. You'd need to be careful."

He sipped his drink. "Honey, are you trying to tell me something?"

"Just to be careful."

"You'd hardly need to tell me that. The police all over the country are keeping an eye cocked for me this minute. If you can help clear me, Lisa, you won't regret it. It would be worth a lot to me."

She reached over and took a cigarette from a box on the cocktail table in front of them. "What could *I* do? What could either of us do against Nannie Koronas?"

"You mean you'd work against him, if you thought it would help?"

"Not for anybody. I would for you, Tom. Aren't you going to light my cigarette?"

He picked up the table lighter and flicked it into flame, and reached over to light her cigarette. Her eyes searched his. "You used to be such a gentleman."

"A lot of good it did me. Doesn't Nannie scare you? You must know him as well as anybody?"

"I know him, and he doesn't scare me too much. Because some of the things I know are in a safe deposit box, to be opened by my lawyer in case I die. Not that Nannie would kill me. He never had it so good."

"You're kidding," Tom said, "aren't you? About the safety deposit box, I mean. You saw that in a movie or in a magazine story, didn't you? It's an old gag."

"It's an old gag and a good one. You're not drinking your drink. Is there something wrong with it?"

Last time, she'd been half-drunk. Last time, she'd been half-drunk and had wanted to climb into the hay. Last time, he'd avoided the hay.

He took a deep swallow. "There isn't a thing wrong with it. It's just the way I like it." He looked at her. "I don't want to get too drunk. You told me to be careful."

"Not around me, Tommy boy. *Everybody* knows I'm out for money. It's the deceitful ones you have to watch out for."

They worked toward the inevitable, drink by drink. The

candy striped dress grew hazier in his vision, her perfume stronger in his nostrils.

Some time during the creeping dusk, he said, "I'd be in great shape if a cop should walk in."

Her voice was soft. "Nobody's going to walk in. *Nobody* has a key."

They were on the davenport, still sitting erectly, but closer, now. The radio was on, softly, and there was a commercial chanting the merits of *Litter-MacCann,* funerals with no hidden charges. Tom thought of *Forest Lawn,* and Lois. Joe, too, was buried at *Forest Lawn.*

"They should have been buried together," Tom said.

"Who? What the hell are you talking about?"

"Nothing. That dress hurts my eyes. It's too bright."

"So? I'll take it off."

Her bed was square, seven feet each way. She looked like a doll in it. A squirming doll, a murmuring doll, an active, elastic, demanding, pulsating, rewarding—and finally quiescent doll.

In the perfumed room, she said quietly, "I sure waited long enough for that. How long, Tom?"

"I'm not following you." Spent, he was, emotionally drained.

"Since we first met, since I first lusted for you."

"You were drunk; you didn't lust for me."

"Hmmmmm." She laid a limp hand on his chest. "Don't tell me how I felt; I was there."

In the big bed, on the silk sheets, his body in complete exhaustion, but his mind working, seeking a mental penetration after the physical.

Perhaps, above her lovely neck, there was nothing to penetrate. But who'd been closer to Nannie?

The phone rang, and she reached out to pick up the instrument off one of the shelves of the headboard. "Hello? Oh —watching TV. Watching what? The wrestling, of course. You know I love wrestling. It isn't on? Well, it certainly looked like wrestling to me." She ran a fingernail along Tom's chest. "Ames, don't be tiresome. Are you *checking* on me? All right, honey; if you get a free minute, phone me."

She sighed as she replaced the phone in its cradle. "Why is

it the least faithful men are the most suspicious?"

"I guess it's called projection. If I had you, I'd be jealous, too."

"Darling, you've just *had* me."

"You know what I mean. If you were mine for good."

"For good? You wouldn't like that. Forever, you mean, and if you were clear, this could be arranged. Because you'd be rich. I need a rich man for the long haul, Tom baby."

"You deserve one. Is this Ames Gilchrist talking wedding bells?"

Her laugh was short and cynical. "It's the furthest thing from his mind." She paused. "Right now."

"Theatrical man? A producer, maybe? A director?"

A longer pause, the kind of pause that precedes a lie. "He's got some influence in the industry. I don't know how much. With men like Ames, it's hard to tell."

Silence growing in the room. Something under the silence, something unvoiced, something important, pounding at the silence.

Tom thought of Lois' words, and paraphrased them. "Is our only communication the physical, Lisa?"

"I'm not with you, baby. Put it in English."

"I'm a convicted murderer. Don't you know anything about that, anything that would help?"

The silence seemed to deepen; the room was a tomb. And then, quietly, hesitatingly, "I can't think of anything. I'd be glad to help, though. There are—there could be things I know that don't seem to be important, now, but—" She took a breath. "It's Nannie, you *do* mean, isn't it, Tom? It's Nannie you suspect?"

"Who else?"

She rose to a sitting position. "Yes, I guess there isn't anyone else. Are you hungry?"

"I could eat."

She sat there a moment, looking down at him. Then, "I lied about Ames Gilchrist, Tom. He's not in the industry. He's one of the boys from the East, one of the boys Nannie is fighting."

"I see. He gets around a lot, doesn't he?"

"What do you mean by that?"

"He—was at another place where I was hiding, a place that has no connection with you or Nannie or my wife. He tried a door that was locked, in his nosy way. I'd locked it, for my protection."

"Where was this, Tom?"

"I don't want to name the place. I don't want the—person involved."

"A girl?"

"Don't pry, Lisa."

"I don't need to, and I'll tell you this, it wasn't just an accident that Ames knows the girl. He looked her up just as he looked me up, though he'd never admit it. He's looking for all the ammunition he can get against Nannie."

Tom said nothing, studying Lisa.

She said, "All right, I've given you that about Ames. Now tell me what you know about Ames."

"Why?"

"Because I want to know if he's using me for a patsy against Nannie. I sure as hell don't mean to be the girl in the middle in this kind of war, Tom."

He smiled. "You want to be the girl on top, don't you? You're going to play along with both of them until you see which one is winning."

She climbed out of bed and started to dress. Then, suddenly, she stopped dressing and stared at the chair nearby. Tom knew what she was staring at. His clothes were on the chair and the .38 on top of them.

Her face was cold as she turned toward him. "You son-of-a-bitch, you certainly came prepared didn't you?"

Chapter 8

HE SAT up in the big bed. "What the hell would you want me to carry, a slingshot? I'm not going back to Missouri, Lisa. Not alive."

She watched him rigidly, the candy-striped dress in her

hand. Finally, she said, "You—scared me, for a second. The gun scared me. You don't look—natural, carrying a gun."

He didn't answer. He slid out of bed and started to dress.

His back was to her, when she asked, "Did you always carry a gun, Tom? When you were working for Nannie, did you—I mean, you and the others—"

"None of us. You know we didn't. Nannie didn't believe in the heavy stuff."

"As far as you know."

He turned to face her. She had the dress on, and was running a comb through her hair. He asked, "What do you mean? Do you know something different about him?"

Lisa looked at him challengingly. "I know he's got a big, fat-faced thug working for him right this minute. I wouldn't be surprised if the man is looking for you."

"A man in a '51 Chev Club?"

"I don't know the year, but it's a Chev Club."

"Sand gray?"

She nodded. "You've seen him? You know him?"

"I've seen him. What's his name?"

"Neilson, Luke Neilson. A Chicago import of Nannie's."

"He didn't look like much to me, big and stupid."

"Of course. Men are so bright about things like that. But I spent too much time in burlesque to judge by looks. And if this Neilson's stupid, it would be the first stupid man Nannie Koronas ever hired."

Tom sighed, and sat on the edge of the bed to put on his shoes. "All right. Yes. What do you like about me, Lisa? I'm not rich."

"You were, and you could be, again. Who says I like you?"

"I've been hiding behind a lot of skirts," Tom went on. "I married money, though I loved her. But when I look in the mirror, it doesn't figure."

"Maybe you're just lucky," Lisa said. "Let's not get studious; this isn't the room for it. I've a pair of fine filets in the refrigerator, lover."

Lisa was quiet, at dinner, subdued. *Three dinners,* Tom

thought, *in three evenings and each one with a different girl, each girl attractive in her way. Stud Spears.*

He thought of Jean Revolt, and the images of the other two faded.

Tom said, "Did you know Joe Hubbard?"

Lisa looked up from her coffee. "Not well. I've met him."

"Through Nannie?"

"Naturally. He did some work for Nannie. I don't travel in the Joe Hubbard circles, Tom." She reached for a cigarette from a pack on the table. "Not yet. Maybe never. If you're wondering, was I one of his women, the answer is 'no.' Though I think he tried, one night at a party."

"He was certainly handsome," Tom said quietly.

"I guess. He simply didn't register with me." She lighted the cigarette and blew smoke toward the ceiling.

"Nannie's probably attractive to women, too, in his way," Tom went on casually.

Nothing showed on her face. "Nannie's rich."

So was Lois, Tom thought, and wondered if he should voice it. And wondered if Lisa knew. And wondered how many other things he hadn't known about his friends, about his wife.

He said, "You're exceptionally quiet. Something's wrong?"

"The gun is wrong," she said. "It scares me. Were you going after Nannie with it?"

"It's for protection only."

"I'll bet." Her voice was strained.

"You don't think I should be armed with a man like Luke Neilson following me around? Lisa, it isn't the gun that's made the difference. Something else is bothering you."

"It's not only the gun, no. It's *you* and a gun. Aren't you in enough trouble, now? Tom, stay away from Nannie Koronas. With or without a gun, stay away from him."

The same warning Jean had given him. But where else could he find the truth of Lois' death? He said nothing.

Lisa was pouring herself another cup of coffee when the door chime sounded. She looked up quickly. "That isn't from the lobby. That's from the hall, up here. I'll bet it's that damned Ames—"

"Do you have to answer it?"

She nodded. "It might even be Nannie. You can hide in that closet off the entrance hall. Come on."

He followed her to the entrance hall. He squeezed in among the coats of the guest closet as she went to the front door.

"Well, Ames, this is unexpected. Come to take me to dinner?"

"If you want." The voice was soft, casual. "Hope I'm not disturbing any of your plans."

"Nothing serious. Go in and mix yourself a drink. I'll get into something a little dressier."

Tom tried to remember if they'd closed the sliding door to the kitchen. If Gilchrist saw the dirty plates on the table, on the table set for two. . . .

Silence. There was a cedar odor in the closet; the soft fur of a jacket was close to his cheek. Silence.

And then Ames' voice: "Are these the lunch dishes in the kitchen?"

"That's right," came dimly from the direction of the bedroom. "Sloppy Lisa. Dinah didn't come today."

"Who was here for lunch?"

"Not Nannie, so don't worry about it."

Silence. Then footsteps on the linoleum of the kitchen floor. And silence again. Then Lisa's voice: "Mix me one while you're at it, Ames."

No answer. Silence.

"Ames—did you hear me?" Her voice sounded louder, closer. "Ames, what in the world are you doing, snooping?"

In Tom's hand, the .38 trembled. He put his other hand out to grasp the doorknob on this side.

From the living room: "Ames, what in the world are you—"

Tom felt the doorknob turn and he lifted the gun in his hand. The door opened, and he faced a tall, blond man dressed in dark blue gabardine.

Gilchrist took a step backward, his eyes on the gun.

Tom said hoarsely. "That's right, keep moving back. You're too God-damned nosy, Gilchrist."

The blond man backed into the entrance hall, his eyes still on the gun. Then Lisa came in from the living room. She stared at the gun, too.

It was Lisa who broke the silence. "Tom, that isn't necessary. Put it away, Tom. You're among friends."

Gilchrist lifted his gaze to meet Tom's and a partial smile came to his tanned, thin face. "That's right. Lisa and I aren't married, you know. We're only friends."

"You might be her friend," Tom said, "but if it's all right with you, I'll pick my own. Don't worry, I'm leaving."

Gilchrist's poise was back. "I'm not worried. But I think you're making a serious mistake about me. I'm on your side."

"Oh? How do you know who I am? We never met."

Gilchrist was silent a moment. Then, "She called you Tom. I guessed the rest. I heard you were in town."

"I'll bet you did. You might even have sent a man to look for me, a man who posed as a cop, huh? That could have been your work. You've got too much nose, Gilchrist."

Gilchrist said evenly, "I don't know what you're talking about. Somebody's been lying to you." He looked away for the first time. He looked at Lisa.

She shook her head. "Not me, Ames. You know it."

Tom said, "How are you on my side, Gilchrist? What do I mean to you?"

"You were one of Nannie's best outlets. And I'll bet he cheated you plenty. To say nothing of sending you to jail. Is that where your loyalty lies, Spears?"

Confidence had returned in force to Ames Gilchrist. His whole attitude was relaxed; his gaze no longer deigned to drop to the gun in Tom's hand.

Tom felt behind him for the front doorknob, his eyes on both of them.

Lisa said, "You're being very stupid, Tom. You're turning down what could be a valuable friend."

"I'll pick my own, as I said before, Lisa. You'd have done better to string with Nannie."

Gilchrist's voice was calm. "Is that who you're sticking with? Have you looked him up, yet, Tom?"

Tom didn't answer. The knob was in his hand, now, and he swung the door open, and stepped out into the hallway. He could see the elevator door was still open, the cage was still at this floor. He moved quickly down that way, his eyes on the open door to Lisa's apartment.

He started to tremble before the elevator had reached the

first floor. He was no gunman; violence sickened him. The edge of his pre-steak drunkenness was now a sour taste in his mouth, the memory of Lisa in that big bed made him feel unclean.

Lois hadn't left him feeling that way. Nor had Jean. Maybe, he thought, I'm semi-moral. Or maybe I'm just fussy.

A steady stream of traffic went by on Sunset. Why hadn't Jud told him Nannie was in trouble? From a drugstore a block down, he phoned Jud again. This time he was home.

"This is Tom, Jud. You all right?"

"What the hell happened to you, Tom? What—where—"

"I'm in a drugstore on Sunset."

"Nannie's been looking for you. He wants to see you."

"I'll bet he does. It's not mutual."

"Are you crazy? What's the story, Tom?"

"I don't know all of it, yet. But I don't want to see Nannie." A silence, and then, "Where are you? I'll pick you up."

"I don't want you to stick your neck out, Jud."

"Let me worry about that."

"And I don't want to see Nannie."

"He won't be with me. Where can I pick you up?"

Tom hesitated, and then gave Jud the address on Kenmore. "I'll be watching for you. It's the rear apartment on the right on the first floor."

He caught a cab at the next corner and took it to within two blocks of the apartment. He came up Kenmore slowly, on the opposite side of the street, scrutinizing all the parked cars he passed and those farther up the block. There was no gray club coupe in sight.

Jud was an organization man, as loyal as a Tammany Democrat. Jud was in the lower echelon; he couldn't be making much more than eighty a week, a workingman's outlet. It would be logical that all he would know about the Eastern infiltration would be through rumor; Nannie didn't confide in the boys at Jud's level.

But Jud was still an organization man and that had been a risk, giving him the Kenmore address. Who else could he trust, though? Jean, he could trust and Delavan. Maybe.

The apartment was as he had left it. From the apartment

102

above came the laughter of a party and the measured tread of a dancing couple.

Delavan had brought milk with the groceries; Tom warmed a glass of it in a small pan and sipped it slowly. When he heard the front door open, he went to the apartment door.

Jud came down the dimly lighted hallway alone, his lanky figure swathed in an oversized topcoat. Jud was always cold at night.

He came in and Tom closed the door.

Jud stood there a moment, looking around the apartment, and then he smiled at Tom. "Cozy. Did you rent it?"

Tom shook his head. "It belongs to a friend. When did Nannie get in touch with you, Jud?"

"Yesterday." Jud reached into one of the topcoat pockets and brought out a fifth of whisky. "Figured you could use a snifter."

"Not now, thanks. What'd Nannie want?"

"He wanted you to get in touch with him. What's happened between you two?"

"I don't know," Tom said. "But I'm not making any moves to get in touch with him until I know more than I do now."

Jud shrugged. "Well, you know him better than I do, Tom. I only saw him once in my life, the first month I worked for him. But he's got a pretty fine reputation. If you don't want a drink, I do. I'll never get used to these California nights." He took the bottle with him to the kitchen.

Tom followed him out. "Didn't you hear any rumors about Nannie getting some competition?"

Jud shook his head. "I heard the heat was on, that's all. Who confides in me?"

"I will. Nannie was—sleeping with my wife."

Jud was peeling the plastic from the cap of the bottle, and he stopped now, to stare at Tom. He opened his mouth, but no words came out.

"That's number one," Tom went on. "And number two is this—he paid Joe Hubbard to come and defend me in St. Louis. And Joe, I've been told by experts, butchered the case. For a lawyer at Joe's level it had to be *deliberate*, the way he butchered the case."

Jud continued to peel away the plastic. "Who told you all these things? *Friends*, Tom?"

"Friends."

Jud removed the cap and poured about an ounce and a half into a small glass. "You're sure of that?" He added some water from the tap.

"I'm as sure of them as I am of Nannie."

Jud sipped his drink, not looking at Tom. "If Nannie's gunning for you, this is a hell of a place for me to be. But it doesn't figure, Nannie gunning for anybody."

"He's hired the gun," Tom said. "A big piece of muscle from Chicago, a man named Luke Neilson."

Jud frowned. "You're wrong on that, Tom. Luke's one of his collectors. He collects from me."

"And follows me. And follows the private investigator who's working for me."

"Investigator? You hired a shamus? Are you crazy? You should know you can't trust those stinking—"

"I can trust this one," Tom interrupted. "Damn it, Jud, I have to trust somebody."

They went into the living room, and Jud sat on the davenport. He leaned forward, his drink in the fingertips of both hands. "I think you can trust Nannie Koronas. Don't ask me why; it's just a feeling I have. I don't know about Nannie and your wife, but if it's true, he wasn't doing anything that others weren't doing." Jud looked up challengingly. "Right?"

Tom nodded.

"Okay, then, maybe some of the others got axes to grind, too. Did that occur to you?"

"What others, Jud?"

"How do I know? Rumors, I get and what you've told me about these 'experts' you're consulting. I don't know who the people are. Whose place is this?"

"A friend's."

"Sure. Maybe. But I don't know him. This I know, Nannie's got dough and influence and he never cheated me out of a dime. You made a good living off of him."

"I brought in a lot of business."

"Sure. Some of these used car salesman bring in business,

104

too. But they didn't make your kind of money."

Tom smiled. "Okay, Jud, you're a party man. You'll ride with city hall. And you think Luke Neilson's only a collector. But two people are dead, one of them my wife. And I was convicted for her death. So maybe I've got more reason to distrust Nannie Koronas than you have."

Jud nodded. "Maybe. And you're my friend. But I won't work against him. For you or anybody else, Tom."

"I'm not asking you to. I'm trying to put together the pieces of a murder puzzle. All I wanted was the pieces you have."

"I've only got one—Nannie wants to see you."

"He didn't want to when I was in jail. He never even wrote me a letter. He didn't come to the trial. His interest in me is kind of late. And doubtful."

Jud finished his drink and stood up. "All right. Then there's nothing more I have to say."

"You can say this—you can tell me you're not going to tell Nannie where I'm staying."

"I told him yesterday I didn't know."

"But if he should ask you again?"

Jud looked at Tom and away. "I'm no pigeon."

Tom smiled. "That's where the pigeons roost, Jud, at city hall."

"What the hell kind of remark was that?"

"A rotten one. I'm sorry, Jud. I'm not forgetting you were the first one I ran to when I came back to town. Don't forget your whiskey."

"You keep it," Jud told him. "I think you're going to need it worse than I will." He went to the door, and out.

Chapter 9

In the apartment above, now, there was more than one couple dancing. They must have rolled back the rug; Tom could hear the slide and beat of their feet on the bare floor.

In the kitchen, he studied the bottle Jud had left and then poured a half ounce into a glass. He sipped it slowly. Cheap whiskey. What loyalty did Jud owe Nannie; he could make as much in the aircraft plants. But he'd have to punch a clock in the aircraft plants.

Jud's loyalty was automatic, like a dog's. Jud was loyal to the man who fed him. When Tom had come to him for haven, Jud had assumed Tom was still one of Nannie's boys. Now that Jud knew he wasn't . . . ? It had been stupid, letting Jud know this address.

Laughter, overhead, the crash of a glass. Tom put the bottle of whiskey into one of the cupboards and went back into the living room to smoke a cigarette.

It was late, and he was tired. Though nights afforded him the cover of darkness, there was the disadvantage of increased police suspicion at night. And the lack of covering daytime crowds.

Besides, where could he go next, except to Nannie? And he had decided against that.

He undressed slowly and filled the bathtub with water as hot as he could bear it. He lay in it until it cooled, seeking solace for his edginess, an external opiate for his growing sense of futility.

The party upstairs was quieting down when Tom climbed into bed. But sleep avoided him; he thought back on all those he'd met since Jean had first brought him back to town. He thought back on what these people had told him and tried to form a pattern from it, a pattern that would point to a killer. What pattern there was seemed to point toward Nannie Koronas.

He would prefer Ames Gilchrist as his personal suspect; there was a man whose background Delavan should check. And the girl, too, Lisa Prentice. She probably knew a lot more than she'd admitted to Tom. He'd talk to Delavan about both of them tomorrow.

He fell asleep thinking about Jean Revolt.

In the morning, he was wakened by the sound of a radio across the hall, a platter program for early morning risers. This didn't seem to be an apartment building where anyone worried about disturbing the neighbors.

The sense of futility he'd taken to bed with him hadn't diminished. He stared at the faded beige paint of the ceiling,

106

wondering if it wouldn't be smart to continue the flight he'd planned when he'd broken from the warden's yard.

But he'd need allies, again, if he wanted to get enough money and the forged credentials necessary to leave the country. Going to Mexico wouldn't be hard; from there it would be possible to go almost anywhere else in the world.

And live *how* the rest of his life? Live in fear the rest of his life? If he had to. Any kind of living outside the walls was better than inside.

He rose and went into the kitchen to put some water in the coffeepot. He turned on a low flame under it and went into the bathroom to shave.

His haggard face stared back at him; even without the glasses it would require some searching to find the pre-prison face of Tom Spears.

He was safe enough from casual discovery; he would be safe in any town where no one was *searching* for him. That would be any town but this one. Run, sheep, run. . . .

He was no sheep. He was a man. Bedraggled and harassed, fearful and sought, a noncombative citizen of an aggressive world. But a man, and he couldn't run away from himself.

He bathed his face with cold water after his shave. He held a cold wet cloth to the back of his neck, striving to chill some of the lethargy from his body and mind.

He made the coffee strong and drank it black. He counted the money in his wallet and learned that he was down to thirty-nine dollars. He would need to buy a few shirts, which would cut his capital still lower.

He dressed and put the .38 in the waistband of his trousers and went out into a gloomy, cool morning. From a filling station phone on Sunset, he called Delavan's number, but there was no answer. Then he called Jean.

She answered almost immediately and he said simply, "Tom. Anything new?"

"Nothing. Have you seen Leonard today?"

"Not since yesterday afternoon. Why?"

"He was coming over last night, and he didn't. Nor did he phone. Are you phoning from that apartment?"

"No. A filling station."

"Tom, you fool!"

"I got sick of sitting. I learned some things. Could I see you?"

"You're in Hollywood?"

"Right. Without a car."

"Go back to the apartment. I have the address. Go back *right now*, Tom."

"Yes, dear. And you be careful."

"Me? Don't worry about *me*."

"I do. I wanted you to know that."

"All right. I know it, now. Go back to the apartment, this second." A pause. "Darling." The click of her phone and a dead line.

He had a fresh pot of coffee made by the time she got there. She came into the living room and stood there quietly, a moment, looking around, and then she looked up at him.

And he was close and he saw her lower lip quaver as she looked up at him, and he took a step and she came to him as though it were the most natural thing in the world.

After a few seconds, he said, "Well, that was—how do they call it? That was —kismet."

"Kismet again," she said. "I liked it. Heavens, that was a horrible pun, wasn't it?" Tremor in her voice.

He pulled her close. "Jean, I guess we—love us, don't we? This isn't anything casual, is it?"

She rubbed her forehead against his cheek. "I'm never casual, unfortunately. It's one of my vices. I wish I could be. I get this Carrie Nation feeling and wonder when I'm going to start *looking* like that, and—Oh, hell, I'm boring you."

"Never. Keep talking."

"I get these—these enthusiasms, these shining CAUSES, this unwomanly urge to tilt at windmills, and think of how dull that would be for a man, a lifetime of *that*. It's probably what kept Joe from—"

"To hell with Joe. Don't talk about that son-of-a-bitch." He kissed her forehead. "I made some coffee. Let's have a cup."

They drank their coffee in the living room and he told about going to Connie Garrity and about Lisa Prentice. He said, "Lisa tells me Nannie was another of Lois' conquests."

She nodded. "I can believe it. And were Connie and Lisa

108

a pair of Tom Spear's conquests?"

"That's not a fair question, honey. We didn't start going together until five minutes ago."

"I don't want another Joe Hubbard," she said quietly.

"Do you think I am? I was true to my wife every minute of our marriage. Easy, baby, you're getting that Carrie Nation look."

She stared at her coffee cup. "What else did the girls tell you?"

"Lisa told me Nannie's getting some Eastern competition, and it's rough competition. One of the boys is Ames Gilchrist. Try that name on for size."

"That—drip, that smeary thing?" Her stare lifted from the coffee cup to fasten on Tom. "He certainly can't be much of a menace."

"Don't judge by looks. The day after he tried the door to that room, a phony cop comes to investigate. I was hiding in Lisa's hall closet when Ames dropped in there. He was just as nosy, again, and he found me in the closet. I had a gun, fortunately."

Her face froze. "And—?"

"And I got away. He tried to talk to me, but I wouldn't listen. This man who parked outside of Connie's and was waiting for Leonard in front of his office is somebody else. His name is Luke Neilson and he works as a collector for Nannie."

"Waiting for Leonard—? Tom, I didn't know anyone was waiting in front of Leonard's office."

"Yesterday afternoon, late. Haven't you heard from him since?"

She shook her head. Silence, while they stared at each other. And then Jean rose. "I'm going over to his office. And his home. You wait right here."

"That's dangerous, Jean. Why don't we sit tight for a while?"

"It's not dangerous. You wait right here. I won't do anything foolish."

"I want to go along." He stood up.

"*That* would be dangerous for me. That would tie me to you. Don't you see, Tom? I'm clear, now. It's best for both
109

of us if I stay clear." She came over to stand next to him. "Kiss me, you philanderer."

He kissed her. He held her close and whispered, "*Former* philanderer. Darling, for God's sake, be careful."

"I promise. And if something has happened to him, I'll go right to the law. I'll tell the police all we've learned. I'll tell them everything except about you. I know quite a few of them in the Department, Tom. I've some standing there, through Dad."

He held her at a distance. "All right. I'll wait two hours. No more than that. I'm ashamed of hiding behind your shield."

She came closer to put her fingertips on his mouth. "Don't ever say that again. We're doing this the sensible way. You're not hiding from anything but injustice. And only temporarily."

"We hope."

"I know. Don't stir, now, until you hear from me, *please.*" She kissed the back of his hand and went to the door. "Wait for me," she said there, and went out.

He warmed the coffee and poured himself another cup. He sat in the living room and listened to the sound of the radio from across the hall. Three days ago, he would have settled for this hide-out; now it was irksome. Jean's work, this change of attitude?

Even Delavan, that realist, could be infected by Jean's dedicated devotion to lost causes. Bucking Nannie Koronas could be a new high in lost causes. Though Ames Gilchrist obviously didn't think so.

And Lisa? No. Lisa was waiting for a winner, staying friendly to both parties at city hall. A scheming little bundle of lust, that Lisa Prentice, and she'd probably be the only one in the melee who'd wind up on top.

He was scrambling some eggs when Jean came back at noon. She told him, "He's not at the office, and his morning paper is still on his front porch. Do you think, Tom, he might have left town on a lead, and not had time to phone me?"

"That could be. How about some lunch?"

She nodded wearily.

"Sit down," Tom told her. "Don't start imagining things that probably didn't happen. He might even be—scared off."

She shook her head. "Not Leonard. He doesn't scare."

"Yesterday, he was scared. He didn't want to face that man in the coupe."

"But he went back, didn't he? That's what I mean." Jean ran a hand over her hair. "I tried to find the superintendent of his office building. I wanted to get a key and check the office. But the man wasn't around. Tom, Leonard was supposed to come over last night. He didn't even phone."

Tom sat down next to her on the davenport. "Don't start imagining things, I told you. We'll hear from him. Would you like me to warm you some milk?"

She patted his hand. "No, thanks. You'd better eat those eggs or they'll turn dry. I'll make my own." She stood up, and smiled down at him. "Back to the wars, baby. I don't scare very often."

"You should. It's a frightening world."

She was at the stove and he was eating his eggs, when she asked, "You didn't tell this Lisa you were staying here, did you?"

"No."

"Or anyone else?"

Tom didn't answer immediately and Jean studied him before saying. "You did. Who, Tom?"

"Jud Shallock. He was here last night."

Jean closed her eyes. "Oh, God!"

"Jud's all right. Don't worry about him. He's loyal to Nannie, but he's no pigeon. Don't lose any sleep over Jud."

"Of course not. Tom, you fool—How in the world did he find you?"

"I phoned him and told him to come over. I wanted to check this story Lisa gave me about Nannie's competition, and learn about this Luke Neilson."

Nothing from her. She brought her eggs over to the table and sat down. She ate quietly, thoughtfully.

"Can't you see it?" Tom protested. "Everybody doing everything for me, and it's *my* neck. I had to do something for myself. What kind of a man would I be if I didn't?"

"A free one. A live one. I'm surprised Nannie Koronas

hasn't sent Neilson here already."

"He doesn't know I'm here. I trust Jud Shallock. I know him."

"All right, all right. *All right!*"

The knock on the door came only a second after her words.

Jean's voice was suddenly shaky. "Leonard, do you think?"

He shook his head. "Leonard has a key. He told me not to answer the door."

"I could answer it, Tom. If it's the police, they'd need a warrant. And if it's the police, they can force an entrance if we don't answer. I'll go. Leonard may have lost his key, or—"

The knock came again.

Tom rose and pulled the .38 from his waistband. He put it in the pocket of his jacket and kept his hand on it. "All right, you go. But be ready to duck. It could be—anybody."

He went over to stand next to the door.

Jean paused a moment with her hand on the knob, and then opened it. With the door open, Tom couldn't see her face, but he could hear the tremor in her voice.

"Yes? What is it?"

"I'm looking for Tom, mam."

"Tom who? Who are you?"

"Luke Neilson's my name, mam. He may not know me. I started working for Nannie after Tom left the organization."

Tom had the gun out, now, and he said quietly to Jean, "All right, honey, let him come in."

Chapter 10

JEAN TOOK two backward steps and the man came in and Tom kicked the door shut behind him.

Neilson turned, his bland gaze going to the gun in Tom's hand and then up to meet Tom's apprehensive glare. Neilson shook his head. "What's the gun for?"

"Protection."

112

"I haven't any gun. Have the lady search me, if you don't believe it. You don't need a gun around me, Tom; I work for Nannie."

"I know it. You're bigger than I am. This gives me the edge. What's happened to Delavan?"

Neilson frowned. "How do I know? I talked to him yesterday. I told him to have you get in touch with Nannie. Didn't he tell you that?"

Tom said quietly, "If you talked to him yesterday, you must have been the last man to see him."

Neilson's face was suddenly guarded. "I left him in his office. Something's happened to Delavan?"

"You know as much as we do, and probably more. Why were you parked in Venice so long?"

"Watching that Garrity broad. I checked her from time to time from the minute we heard you'd made the break. Joe's best girl, wasn't she? And isn't Joe the key to this thing? Were you there, at the Garrity girl's joint? You never showed."

"I'll ask the questions," Tom said. "I've got the gun. Who told you I was here?"

"Nannie."

"And who told Nannie?"

"I don't ask him those kind of questions."

Jean said hoarsely, "We know who told him. Jud Shallock told him. He was supposed to be Tom's friend."

Neilson's glance went between them and settled on Tom. "What makes her think he isn't your friend, Tom? Are you sure you know who your friends are?"

"I used to think so."

"Sure. Like Joe Hubbard, that shyster. Nannie sent him to St. Louis to defend you. You know that, don't you, now? Nannie paid for that."

"And ordered him to throw me to the wolves."

Again, the bland face frowned. "You can't believe that. We won't talk about Joe Hubbard. He's dead. And there are things Nannie has to say to you he won't trust me with, or anybody else. Just look back over your career with him, Spears, and then start figuring your friends over again from that angle. You can't be too stupid, the regard Nannie's got for you."

113

"There are two reasons," Tom said quietly, "why I'm not going to talk to Nannie just yet. Both of them are buried out at Forest Lawn."

"He'll talk about that, too. You owe it to him, Tom. Nannie's a sick man."

"My wife's worse than that; she's dead. And I was framed for her killing. And you track me around town, working for Nannie. Well, it looks to me like he's gone heavy, and that scares me."

Neilson stared at the gun in Tom's hand. "It looks to me like you're the one that's gone heavy. So, there's another man looking for you, too. And he's armed. And he *doesn't* work for Nannie. You're playing it real stupid, Spears. But it's your neck."

He turned his back on the gun and reached for the door.

Tom said, "You can tell Nannie that I know about him and Lois. I know a hell of a lot more than he gives me credit for. And when I get enough, the police will know it."

Neilson looked at him almost pityingly. "Cops. Now we're hollering cops. Stupid, I know you are, now, but a stoolie—? Nannie sure had you pegged wrong."

He went out, and slammed the door behind him.

Jean stared at the door for seconds. "Do you still trust Jud Shallock?"

"Jud's an organization man. I'm sure he thought it was the best for me."

"Or for the organization. Maybe they've worked out some kind of deal, Tom. Maybe they can clear you with some cooked up evidence, some shenanigans, prove you didn't kill your wife. And you'd be free."

"Maybe. She wasn't much. But she was my wife. I want to know who killed her. I want the law to know."

Her smile was bitter. "You've come over to my side?"

"I was a bookie," Tom said softly. "Never any more than that. It's illegal, but millions don't think it's immoral. When was I ever on any side but yours?"

She didn't answer that. She stared at him a moment and then she whispered, "Would you kiss me, please, Tom Spears?"

The slim body close, the light perfume soothing and then his cheek was damp from her tears and he stood back.

114

"What now? Why do you cry?"

"Oh—you and the gun. The lamb with the gun. Why should the lambs have to carry guns?"

He didn't answer.

"What if he'd made a move for you, Tom? Could you have pulled the trigger?"

"I don't know. But neither did he. It was all the edge I needed at the moment, his doubt. You're no tiger, yourself, Miss Jean Revolt."

"I'm beginning to find that out." She rubbed at her wet cheek with the back of one hand. "Well, this haven is now lost. You'd better come home with me."

"He knows you, too, now. I mean Neilson does."

"Didn't he before? Who sent that other man to my place, the one who pretended to be a detective?"

"Ames Gilchrist, I think. There's a battle on, Jean, and we're in the middle of the battleground."

Jean picked up her purse. "We mustn't waste any time. I suppose if Joe worked for Nannie, Nannie knows about me. But I've a better hiding place in the house. There's an entrance to the attic through that closet in Dad's study. It leads to a separate wing of the house. You couldn't live up there; the roof's too low. But you could be safe there if somebody came."

"And cornered, if somebody should discover it. I like open ground around me, Jean."

"There isn't any open ground left. Not with two thugs and the police looking for you. Let's hurry, Tom."

It was still gloomy out, and cool. The Plymouth at the curb was the only parked car in the block. "We're clear enough so far," Jean commented. "Those glasses do change your looks. You don't look like a bookie, at all."

"I'm not," Tom said. "Not any more."

There was some mist in Santa Monica, deepening as they came toward Ocean Avenue. She turned right on Ocean, traveling to its end, following the steep road down to Entrada in the Canyon.

In the Canyon, the fog was heavy enough to slow traffic to a crawl; visibility was no more than ten feet. It didn't

115

improve as they climbed toward Jean's house on the other side of Entrada.

She was moving in low gear, her gaze concentrated on the unseen road ahead. "Don't you hate fog?"

"I don't mind it. I lived in it for years."

"Where? In Frisco?"

"No, with Lois. Joke."

"You and millions of others. How about me?"

Tom thought of Connie Garrity's scorn, and the scorn Connie claimed Joe Hubbard had felt for Jean. He said, "Joe was the man in the fog. He didn't know when he had a good thing."

"Thank you, Thomas Spears. It was a gallant thought, but the reality is that Joe had a lot of good things, which is even better, isn't it?"

"I don't know. I'm monogamous by nature."

Nothing from her. The car jolted as she rode too close to the edge of the drive. Around them, now, an almost indistinguishable thinning of the mist as they came to the clearing about the house. Above them towered the mist-shrouded ghost of the giant eucalyptus tree that dominated the parking area.

"Safely home, anyway," Jean said, and turned to look at him. "To paraphrase Stevenson, home is the hunted, high on a hill." A pause. "That was a poor joke. But so was yours about Lois."

He climbed out and waited for her and they went across the macadam of the parking area together.

As she was unlocking the door, she asked, "Are we any closer, Tom? Are we any closer to the truth than we were the day I picked you up in Arizona?"

"Some. Maybe the murderer isn't in sight, but we've certainly learned enough, haven't we, about our—friends?"

She pushed the door open. "Nothing I enjoyed learning. And quite possibly nothing that will do us any damned good."

He patted her cheek. "That doesn't sound like you. That sounds like me. Are we exchanging characters?"

They were in the entry hall, and Tom closed the door. "You've lost nothing, Jean. If I took off, tomorrow, you wouldn't be in trouble."

116

She faced him bleakly, her eyes searching his.

He smiled. "Don't look at me like that. I couldn't leave you. I was talking about your involvement in my *trouble*, not in me. You are clear of the trouble, you know. Nobody could prove you helped me."

"Nobody but Leonard. I wonder where he is?"

"He'll be around. Let's see that attic hideaway."

The entrance to the attic through the study closet was above some shelves and the shelves were strong enough to serve as steps. Tom clambered up and lifted the plywood door. This part of the attic was about four feet high and walled off from the rest of the low attic by the mammoth chimney that served the fireplaces in the living room and study.

Tom came down again and Jean said, "The obvious entrance to the attic is through that opening in the hall ceiling. This one can't even be seen from the floor, you'll notice."

"The police are pretty thorough, Jean."

"If they have reason to be. I didn't get a chance to finish my coffee at that apartment. Would you like some?"

"I guess."

Jean went out. From the mantel, Walter Revolt looked at Tom and there seemed to be some challenge in the pugnacious face. Through the windows, Tom could see the wall of mist, and the drip of moisture from the eaves was audible in the muffled quiet.

Jean was dispirited and perhaps the disappearance of Leonard Delavan was the big factor in that. Leonard had been her strong right arm, her legs, her detecting eye. Leonard had been her lion; she was left with her lamb.

He was standing by the window, looking out at the fog, when she came to tell him the coffee was ready.

In the dim kitchen, he sat in the ell of the fireplace. He sipped his black coffee and smoked and thought back on the hours and events since he had last sat here.

Jean said, "What kind of a girl is that Connie Garrity?"

"Oh—cynical, I guess. She thinks you're a suspicious character. Not that you're a card-carrying Commie, of course, *but*—"

"But I'm a registered Republican, and Dad was, too. But

117

we have to work to maintain freedom. That's the hell of it. We fight for a principle and in fighting for it, are forced to protect some scum."

"Maybe," Tom said, "what you save isn't worth the fight."

"Freedom?"

"No, Tom Spears, for example. You can't fight forever, Jean."

"Everybody fights as long as he lives," she answered. "He either fights for what he believes in or he fights his conscience." She managed a smile. "Do you see what you'd have to live with, Tom Spears, if you married me? Do you see why Joe Hubbard didn't?"

"I don't want to hear about Joe Hubbard, Jean. I don't ever want to hear his name again from you."

"He was no worse than a million others, honey."

"Yes, he was. Because he could have been so much better. That's enough on that bastard, now."

Her eyes looked less weary. "Yes, darling. Yes, boss."

They sipped their coffee and smoked and the fog shrouded them from the sound of traffic and a view of the rest of the world.

Tom said, "I wish I had a crystal ball. I'd like to know where I'd be a month from now."

"Nearer the window," she said. "I'll move this table back near the window after you're cleared, and we'll have a view when we eat."

"*After* I'm cleared—are you still that confident, Jean?"

She started to answer, and then stopped. There was some moisture in her eyes. "I—oh, God, Tom, I don't know—— What could have happened to Leonard?"

He shrugged. "Why don't you phone?"

She nodded and rose. "I will."

He poured himself another cup of coffee and lighted a cigarette. Jean came back in. "No answer. I wish that damned fog would lift."

Tom said, "Take it easy, honey. He could be chasing a very hot lead."

"It only takes a minute to phone. And Leonard is meticulous about keeping appointments." She poured herself a half

118

cup of coffee. "I don't remember ever having the jitters like this, before, Tom."

"You never tried to buck Nannie Koronas before. Even the Kefauver Committee gave up on him."

She lifted her chin. "You still admire him, don't you? You've never really lost that sense of loyalty."

"I don't admire him, except in his field. For a man outside the law, he has standards of his own beyond the others. He has a certain—integrity. He'll never let an employee down."

Her smile was cynical. *"Never—?"*

"So far as I know. He might—"

He stopped talking as Jean suddenly raised a warning hand. He looked at her questioningly.

She whispered, "Didn't you hear that noise? It was a car motor."

Tom listened, and it was audible now, a car moving in one of the lower gears, and coming up the drive.

"Get to that room," she said. "It could be Leonard, but we can't take any chances." She rose swiftly and took the coffee cups and the ash tray over to the sink. She was emptying the ash tray into the garbage grinder as Tom left the kitchen.

In the study, he locked the door behind him and stood close to it, listening.

Nothing for minutes, and then Jean's footsteps coming down the hall. "Tom, the car left again. What do you think it could mean?"

"I don't know. Maybe someone left a message. Or it could be a car that got lost and used your driveway to turn around in."

"I'm going out, Tom, to the mailbox. You wait here, and keep the door locked. If I'm talking when I come in, again, get right up into that attic. Understand?"

"Yes. Do you think it's safe, going out into that fog?"

"I'll be all right."

"If anything happens, scream. I'll come out, with the gun. Remember that, Jean."

"All right. Wait, and listen."

Her footsteps going down the hall, and silence. She evi-

119

dently hadn't closed the front door behind her; he would have heard it from where he stood.

And then, after a minute, her footsteps on the bricks of the patio and they were running. She was still running when she entered the house and came down the hall.

She pounded with a flat hand on the door. "Tom, open up, open up."

He opened the door and saw the near-hysteria on her face. He pulled her close. "What is it, honey?"

"It's Leonard. He's lying out there on the patio. There's nobody around, out there. I—" She started to cry.

"Is he dead?"

"I don't know. I saw him and got panicky. I'd better phone the police."

"I'll go out, first. We want to be sure about him. He may come around. Was there any blood?"

"I didn't see any. Tom, do you think the—whoever, whatever it was, do you think it's still out there?"

Tom took the gun from a shelf in the bookcase. "I'll go out and see."

Jean inhaled and stood stiffly. "I'll go along."

Together, they went out into the fog and along the walk to the brick patio. The blob that was Leonard Delavan got clearer as they approached it.

Then Tom knelt and felt for the pulse. Above him, he could hear the rasp of Jean's labored breathing.

She asked, "Is he—?"

Tom looked up and nodded. "He's dead, Jean."

Chapter 11

In the house, he told her, "Explain everything just the way it happened, except for my being here. And tell them you had hired Leonard to investigate Joe Hubbard's death. Don't mention me, except in my relationship to Joe. I'll get out, now."

"No, Tom, please. That attic is the safest place you could be now. Don't forget, *I'm phoning them.* That cuts down their suspicion about you considerably. And we don't even know the police have any suspicion about you being here. Get up there, Tom, and I'll phone them." She looked up pleadingly. "I want you close. And when they're gone, I want you here."

He leaned forward to kiss her forehead. "All right. Check the room carefully for anything I might have missed."

He was crouched on the two-by-sixes of the attic, his back against the brick of the chimney when he heard the fog-muffled wail of the siren on Channel Road.

A little after that there were footsteps outside and the slam of the front door and then the indistinguishable murmur of conversation from below.

The law was finally in this thing. And with what Jean would give them, Nannie Koronas would come under police scrutiny. *Possibly* that would break it wide open, but *probably not*. Nannie was a past master at cover and concealment. Though covering a murder was a far more difficult job.

Tom's bad knee began to throb and he eased it gently to a less cramped position, conscious of his balance every precarious second. A noise from above would certainly be investigated from below.

There was the sound of another siren. Coming for the body, undoubtedly, the lifeless body of Leonard Delavan. Nannie's work, again? The work of Nannie's new right arm, Luke Neilson?

The throb in Tom's knee grew, but he hesitated to move it again. It sounded, now, as though the conversation was coming from directly below.

On a rafter above him, a fat and shining black widow spider seemed to be studying him. Then it began to move across the roof over his head. It was out of his line of vision, now.

If it continued on the same path, it would be stopped by the chimney. There, it had two choices: up toward the roof or down toward Tom Spears.

Outside, there was the sound of a car engine starting and the closing of a car door. Tom's scalp began to itch; he was certain something was crawling in his hair.

121

He didn't move his head, nor move a hand toward his head; the thing wouldn't bite unless attacked or crowded. He tried to take his mind from it, tried to force his mind to the significance of Leonard's death. But his skin crawled; his mind refused to move away from the plight of Tom Spears.

From below, there was the sound of the front door closing, but conversation continued. Tom pulled at the front of his shirt, trying to pull taut the open collar, to close any apertures that might attract the thing.

Silence, now, from below? Silence. Outside, another car motor coughed into life. On Tom's neck, a light brush, light as a spider's leg. He didn't move. He didn't breathe.

Conversation started up again below. Overhead, a jet plane roared and the shock wave trembled through the house. On Tom's neck, the weight was heavier now; it was crawling around the top edge of his collar.

It came to his chin, and paused. He tried to see it, but it was still outside his line of vision. He moved his right hand slowly up into his lap, ready for a time when he could brush the thing off in one certain motion.

Again the front door opened and closed and now the silence below seemed complete. The weight was on his chin but there was no movement. If it moved toward his eye, toward his mouth, he would have to take the chance of striking at it.

Footsteps below, coming along the hall. Then, from directly below, Jean's quiet voice. "All right, Tom."

He didn't move. He didn't answer. If he answered, he would need to move his jaw.

Her voice was louder. "Do you hear me, Tom? Answer me."

The brushing of a thread like leg; no other movement. "Tom, what's the matter?"

He moved his hand from his lap and started it backward, so he could strike from behind. But the action pulled his shoulder back and the open front of his collar widened. He brought his upper arm in close to his body, bending his hand backward at the wrist.

When his fingertips were even with his shoulder, he moved the hand swiftly, cupping the fingers and brushing savagely

122

from the side of his neck forward.

The spider shot to the top of the plywood in front of him. It scrambled a moment and then Tom's leg lifted and he pulled off a shoe.

He smashed it a moment before it would have disappeared over the corner of a two-by-six.

"Tom——!"

"I'm all right, now," he called. He lifted the plywood covering the attic entry and looked down at her. "There was a black widow on my jaw. I was afraid to move or talk."

"My God!" She put a hand on the closet wall. "Where is it, now?"

"I killed it." He put his shoe back on and moved achingly over to the entry hole. He dangled a moment until his feet found one of the shelves and then he came down to stand beside her.

She was pale; she stared at him sickly. He put his arms around her and drew her close. "Bad day, honey. There'll be better ones."

She said nothing. A shiver passed through her slim body and she clung tightly to Tom. She began to sob. Through the high windows of the study, Tom could see the fog still pressing in around the house.

Tom thought back to the scene in the apartment when Leonard had said, "Maybe this is one of my gutless afternoons." Leonard hadn't wanted to face Luke Neilson.

Jean said, "Leonard was working for me, Tom. He'd be alive if he hadn't been working for me."

"You were paying him, but he was working for me, Jean, to clear me. And yesterday afternoon, he didn't want to go back and face Neilson. Leonard was getting——" He stopped.

She lifted her wet face. "Getting scared? But he went ahead, didn't he? I'm scared, too, Tom."

"I'm not. Because I've everything to gain. Did you tell the police about Nannie?"

She nodded. "And they asked about you. I didn't tell them about this afternoon and Luke Neilson. I couldn't very well, without telling them about you."

"But they asked if you'd seen me?"

She nodded. "So I'm on record as a liar. Tom, do you

believe Neilson was telling the truth when he said he left Leonard at the office?"

"Who knows? Let's sit down, honey. I'll make you a drink. That's what you need."

She sat in the leather chair while he went out to the kitchen. She was staring at her father's picture when he left the room; she was still staring at it when he returned with a small glass of brandy.

He touched her shoulder, and she looked up. He handed her the brandy. "Try to relax." He took his over to the day bed and sat on the edge.

She turned her head to face him. "Why did they——? It—— was a sort of——warning, I suppose, bringing Leonard's body here?"

"Probably. Or a way to get the police to investigate you." He took a breath. "And thus discover me."

"Who'd want you discovered?"

"The murderer. It's better for him if I'm locked up for the crime instead of out hunting him."

She sipped her brandy, holding it in her mouth. She leaned her head back, and closed her eyes. "We've nobody now, Tom. *Nobody*."

"We've us. We've me. And the .38. Even Nannie isn't immune to a .38."

She kept her eyes closed. "That won't do it. A gun never solves anything."

"Guns have solved a lot of problems. How did Leonard die? Had he been shot?"

"He was shot in the back, in the spine. With a fairly small caliber; they think it was a .32. I had to listen to all that." She opened her eyes, staring at the picture of her father again.

Tom sensed that the horror of this day had been its own anaesthetic, numbing her mind.

She said quietly, "That damned fog. It never before has lasted all day. Never, since we moved here, have we had a fog like this, *all day*."

"Get hold of yourself, Jean. Look ahead, not back."

"Ahead to what——?" She turned to stare at him dully. "What can *we* do, Tom? Without Leonard."

"If we can't do anything, I'll get out of town. But I intend to stay with it for a while." He paused. "It's *my* neck."

In the big leather chair, her body shook and one hand pressed desperately on the padded arm. "*I* hired Leonard. *I* came to talk you out of running away."

"Leonard was for hire. It was his job and he knew its risks. Accepting the employment was *his* idea; he wasn't so poverty-stricken he was forced to accept it." Tom paused. "And I'm glad you talked me out of running away. I'm so glad we met."   .

Nothing from her. She sipped her drink, looking out into the room at nothing. She seemed huddled and small in the huge chair.

"I think you'd better take a sedative and lie down," Tom suggested. "You should rest if you can."

She shook her head. "I can't risk it. They'll be back, with questions, I'm sure."

"They're not going to break in if you don't answer the door. Jean, you mustn't crack up. And you mustn't take any blame for Leonard's death. He was a free agent."

Her face was blank. "Don't worry, I'll rationalize that away. In time. Meddler, that's all I am, a meddler."

"No, honey, a citizen. And that takes some meddling these days. Nothing you did was wrong. *Nothing.*"

From the direction of Channel Road came the hysterical shriek of suddenly applied brakes, and Jean jerked in the chair.

Traffic would be stacked up today along here; the Coast Road would be bedlam at going-home time. Tom finished his drink and came over to take the empty glass from Jean's tight grasp.

He took both glasses to the kitchen and then made sure the front door was locked. He came back to the study and said, "Lie down. If you don't want to go to bed, lie on the couch over there. But you have to relax. Please, Jean."

She looked at him and rose obediently. She went over to the couch and lay on her side, and Tom covered her with a blanket.

She said, "There are some sleeping pills in the medicine closet in my bathroom. And a half glass of water, please?"

Fifteen minutes later, she was asleep. Tom sat in the kitchen, looking out at the fog, trying to fit the death of Leonard Delavan into the pattern that had started forming in St. Louis.

So far as he knew, Neilson had been the last man to see Leonard. And Neilson worked for Nannie.

Outside, the fog was thinning. The afternoon shift of wind was blowing it out to sea. Tom rose and went over to turn a low flame under the coffee. As he was reaching for a cup from the cupboard, he saw Jean's car keys on the tile of the drainboard.

What had he brought her but trouble? He could take her car right now, while she slept, and drive to Nannie's. He had the gun, and there was the car.

But that would leave Jean alone and asleep. A dead man had been found on her patio today and she would waken to an empty house. He couldn't desert her now.

He poured a cup of coffee and sat near the window, watching the fog slowly disperse, opening an increasing vista. If only the fog in his mind would clear as well.

Three dead and no solid leads to any of them. Three dead, his wife, his friend and Leonard Delavan. Neilson knew Tom had stayed in that apartment at Kenmore. Neilson had seen Jean there. If Neilson took that to the law and the law learned, as they would, that the building belonged to Leonard . . . ? The law would have a prime suspect for the death of Leonard Delavan, a convicted killer on the loose, a man named Spears.

But Neilson wouldn't be running to the law. He was one of Nannie's boys. As Joe had been. As Jud was, and Jud had betrayed him to Nannie; there'd been no personal loyalty to Tom Spears.

Neilson had given no indication of recognizing Jean. Nor had Tom ever seen the gray coupe parked around here. If Nannie knew he was here, wouldn't he have tried to contact him here? A lead?

Delavan had been dumped *here*. A lead? Not at the apartment on Kenmore, not at Connie Garrity's, not in Delavan's office. All three places Nannie knew about. These three places Neilson had been, but never *here*.

126

Nannie would know about this place, now. The police would question him about it. But there was reason to assume that Nannie hadn't know about it before. Ames Gilchrist had known about this place; the doorknob trying was more than mere nosiness.

In the living room, the phone rang. Tom sipped his coffee and stared out at the clearing fog. In his mind there was the beginning of a pattern as nebulous as the drifting rags of the fog. The phone continued to ring.

Then there were light footsteps in the hall and Tom turned to see Jean coming from the study in her stockinged feet. She smiled at him weakly and turned out of view into the living room.

"Hello. Yes, this is Miss Revolt. Who is this, please?"

A silence of ten to fifteen seconds and then, "I have no idea where he is, Mr. Koronas. And if, through some chance, I should see him, I certainly wouldn't recommend his coming to see you."

A shorter silence, and then, "I have nothing further to say, Mr. Koronas."

The phone began to ring again a few seconds after she entered the kitchen. She poured a cup of coffee, and took it over to the table. Tom came over to sit near her.

"The fog's clearing," he said. "You shouldn't have got up, Jean."

"I wasn't sleeping well. Your Mr. Koronas informs me he's a sick man. And he wants to see you. He has information for you. If he has, why doesn't he give it to the police?"

"Nannie doesn't work with the police. I don't think Delavan's death was his doing. And maybe the others weren't, either. I've *never* known Nannie to play it heavy."

"Think of all the things you've learned the last few days that you *never* knew before. We're not ready to go to Nannie, Tom. When we are, the police will be along."

Tom's voice was gentle. "Will we ever be ready for that, Jean? Aren't you the one who said problems must be faced, not run from? Nannie's our major problem at the moment."

"And we're not ready to face him."

Tom stared at the tablecloth. "I was going to leave, take your car and leave while you were asleep. But I couldn't

127

desert you. Those records you have gave us less than I learned from the people I've talked to since I was here before. Any important records aren't on paper; they're in the memories of the people I met.

"And one other—Nannie Koronas."

"That's right. And he wants to talk to me. He's wanted to ever since I broke from prison."

"But not before. Why not *before*, Tom? Why didn't he come to see you?"

"I don't know. I could ask him."

"Maybe that's what Leonard asked him."

Tom said patiently, "You don't like Nannie Koronas and you'd like to pin everything on him because of that. Maybe it's because you think it was Nannie who corrupted Joe Hubbard. I think Joe double-crossed Nannie. And I think Ames Gilchrist is responsible for Leonard's death."

Jean traced an aimless design on the tablecloth with a finger. Her voice was weary. "You want to talk to Nannie, don't you?"

"Not right away. I want to take your car and go out and see some people. If I get caught, I'll claim to have stolen the car. This isn't a town where I want to rely on public transportation."

Jean said nothing, nor did she look up.

"I want to be sure you're safe, first," Tom said. "I want you to get some friends here or move in with friends."

She looked up and shook her head. "I'll go with you. You haven't even a driver's license."

"You're not going along, Jean. I waited, because I want to be sure you'll be safe. If you don't think I should use your car, I'll go without it. But I'm working alone on this."

She studied him for seconds. Then she said, "I'll pack an overnight bag. You can drop me off at some friends in Santa Monica."

He shaved while she phoned the friends and packed a bag. He put the .38 back into the waistband of his trousers and stood in the kitchen looking out at the now clear day. There would still be an hour or two of sun but he didn't fear casual detection. And the night would be no cover from anyone who was looking for him.

Jean came out from the bedroom with a grip and smiled at him. "You're different. You're——" She shrugged.

"I'm Dick Tracy. I'm a sheep with a wolf's fangs. Perhaps you'd better phone the police from where you're going and tell them you won't be home."

"I will. You're—*resolute*; that's the word I wanted." He kissed her. "I'm your boy."

On Montana, in Santa Monica, he dropped her off in front of a large and old Spanish house. She held his face in her hands and kissed him savagely. She said, "Please be very, very careful. And God bless you, darling."

She turned quickly away and went up to the house without looking back.

He headed the Plymouth south, toward Culver City. It was almost dinnertime and traffic was heavy, the traffic officers out in force. He maintained a speed only a few miles above the legal limit and gave all his attention to the traffic.

Jud's sun-faded Merc convertible was parked in front of the dark gray stucco triplex. There were no suspicious cars parked anywhere near. Tom drove a block past, and walked back.

Jud came to the door with a spatula in his hands, a dish towel protecting the front of his trousers. He looked at Tom hesitantly and then said, "Better come inside. I've some taters frying."

Tom went in and followed him to the kitchen. "I suppose you heard about Leonard Delavan?"

Jud nodded. "From Neilson. The law should be here any minute. This is no place for you."

"You told Nannie where I was, didn't you?"

Jud turned the sliced potatoes over in the pan and reached for a couple of eggs. "I did. For your own good. Come to get me for it, Tom?" He looked up, smiling.

Tom said nothing. Jud broke the eggs over the frying potatoes. "Home cooking, that's what I like. What's on your mind, Tom?"

"I wondered if Neilson killed Delavan."

"He didn't say. Want me to ask him?"

"I'll ask him. I've got a gun, and I'll ask him."

Jud didn't look at him. He reached over and turned off the

flame under the perking coffee. "I heard about the gun, too. I heard you're getting to be a real tough guy."

"But I don't scare you, do I?"

Jud shook his head. "I know you, Tom. You belong with a gun like I belong with the Christian Endeavor. What good's a gun against Nannie? He's too sick to worry about guns, I heard today. He knows what it is, now."

"What is it?"

"The sawbones called it carcinoma. I guess you can translate that, can't you? What the hell do you think can scare Nannie, now?" Jud's face was grim. "All he worries about is his boys, trying to keep the organization solvent and safe for the rest of us. If you've got a gun, Tom, don't pull it on me. I'll make you eat the God-damned thing."

Jud's face was rigid in anger. "I saved your neck the first time. That was before you started hanging around with the competition and then with that bastard Hubbard's girl friend. Don't worry, Tom; I've been getting the story on you."

"Relax, Jud. What the hell are you all wound up about? This is Tom Spears, remember? Your buddy."

"If you're a buddy of mine," Jud said, "you'll go up and see Nannie with me."

"All right, I'll go. He sure gets a lot of loyalty from you for a crummy eighty bucks a week."

"That's right. I'm cheap. But loyal." Jud turned off the flame under the frying pan. "Let's go."

"What's the hurry? Aren't you going to eat?"

"I can always eat. You've been overdue at Nannie's for three days."

Outside, Tom said, "We'd better take my car. The local law knows yours, don't they?"

Jud nodded. "And they'll probably be looking for me. That County man is still suspicious."

As they walked the block to the Plymouth, Jud was quiet, his whole attitude unnatural and strained. Tom had never before seen Jud as emotionally disturbed as he'd been in the kitchen. Perhaps Nannie was all Jud had to believe in.

In the car, Jud lighted a cigarette and said nothing.

Tom headed for Sepulveda and on that busiest of the streets, turned toward Wilshire Boulevard. Jud smoked quietly.

As they stopped for the light on Olympic, Tom said, "Nannie must be confiding in you more than usual, lately."

"I was his only contact with you." Jud opened the window and threw the cigarette out. "And you're his fair-haired boy. I wouldn't be surprised if he meant for you to inherit the organization. He hasn't got any kids, you know."

"I'm out of the organization," Tom said.

"You're telling me. Out of *this* one."

"And all like this one. I've booked my last bet, Jud."

Nothing from Jud. On Wilshire, Tom turned right, toward Westwood. He said, "My wife is dead. A man I thought was my friend is dead. Now Delavan's dead. I'm supposed to come back to town and run trustingly to Nannie, the man who sent Hubbard to double-cross me, the man who was making time with my wife. He had his big muscle man trail me around town. He had him approach Delavan. Have you ever thought maybe *you're* wrong about Nannie, Jud?"

"Wait until you see him." Jud continued to look straight ahead. "You've been mixing in some strange company. Wait until you talk to an honest man for a change."

On the street before Westwood Boulevard, Jud said, "Turn left here."

They turned off into the quiet backwater of Westwood Village, right to the Boulevard and then out toward one of the winding streets that climbed to the view lots northeast of the UCLA campus.

Nannie's place was modern, an expansive, one story showplace of flat roofs and glass brick. Tom turned in at the green macadam drive, keeping an eye open for Department cars.

There were none in sight as he drove around to the parking area in the rear. It held no cars; through the open garage doors, Tom could see Nannie's Mercedes and his Cad.

Jud said, "Maybe I'd better go to the door alone, first. There might be some flatfeet hiding in the woodwork."

Tom said jestingly, "I didn't know you cared, Jud."

"I don't, but Nannie does." Jud climbed out and slammed the car door behind him.

In a minute, he was back, and he nodded and waved for Tom to come. He waited for Tom at the door.

Tom followed him through an entry hall and down a longer hall that led to an enormous laboratory-like kitchen. Nannie sat in a magnesium and plastic chair in front of a black plastic dining table.

Tom couldn't disguise the sharp intake of his breath the sight of Nannie brought. The man's face was skull-thin; his clothes were voluminous on his emaciated frame. His pale lips bent in a smile at sight of Tom, and he half rose to hold out his hand.

Tom hesitated for only a second before taking it. He noticed that one of Nannie's hands was on the table in front of him, supporting him. His voice was firm and clear, though.

He said, "It's about time, Tom. It's about time you looked up your best friend. Is that a gun in your belt, Tom?"

Tom nodded. "It's what will keep me from going back. I'm never going back, Nannie."

Nannie nodded, saying nothing.

Tom said, "I didn't look you up, because you didn't look me up, when I was in that place, Nannie. I never had a word from you."

"I know. I know, Tom. We'll talk about that later." He looked at Jud. "When we're alone. But first, we must give Jud some dinner. I suppose you haven't eaten?"

"It can wait," Jud said. "Your talk's more important than my dinner. I'll wait in the car."

Nannie shook his head. "Go into my study, Jud. I'll have some dinner sent in to you. Steak do it, boy?"

Jud's smile had some collie quality. "It sure will, boss. It's a long step up from the grub cooling in my frying pan this second."

Jud went out, and Nannie said, "Great boy. He won't regret his loyalty when he sees the will. Great underpaid boy."

A man who looked like an ex-fighter came in. He wore a white jacket. Nannie talked to him in sign language, and the man said, "Got it, boss. I'll fix him good."

"Deaf," Nannie explained to Tom. "Got him a couple of months ago. Great cook. And he used to be a male nurse. I've always been lucky with help, haven't I, Tom?"

Tom had seated himself in a twin of Nannie's chair on the

132

far side of the table. He nodded. "I guess you have. You've been on top a long time."

"Something to eat?" Nannie asked.

Tom shook his head and looked at the glass of milk in front of Nannie.

Nannie looked at it, too, and then shoved it away. "Tom, first about not coming to see you, not writing you, not sending anyone. I couldn't. You see, I was in love with your wife, and we'd——"

"I know about that," Tom interrupted. "You weren't the first."

"No, but I didn't know that at the time. We were going to be married, Tom, if you'd give her a divorce. That's how I felt about Lois."

The truth? Nannie's voice was steady as his gaze and Nannie had never been a liar. Tom looked away.

"I suppose," Nannie went on quietly, "I should have come to you as soon as we were—sure. Tom, I didn't have that kind of guts, knowing how you loved her. I——"

On top of the table, Nannie's bony hand clenched and his wasted face screwed up in pain, his eyes closed. He opened his eyes and took a deep breath. "So, I talked to Joe Hubbard about it, thinking he might approach you. He was such a good friend of yours, I thought."

"So did I," Tom said bitterly.

"Yes, yes." Nannie held up a hand. "We'll get to that. Anyway, before Joe talked to you, Lois was killed. I thought you'd done it, having learned about—us, about Lois and me. I sent Joe to St. Louis to defend you and told him to hire the best help in the business. He butchered the case, I learned later. And when I accused him of it, he got panicky and claimed he'd thought that was what I wanted him to do. At first, I believed him. And then I learned he'd—been a friend of Lois' too." Nannie paused, looked at the man in front of the stove for a moment, and then back at Tom. "So I shot Joe, I killed him. The first time I'd ever shot a gun, Tom, and it's nothing I'll ever forget."

Silence in the kitchen except for the sizzle of the steak.

Tom said softly, "But who killed Lois?"

133

Nannie shrugged. "I don't know. I thought you had. You didn't, Tom?"

Tom shook his head slowly, staring at Nannie.

Nannie said, "It isn't too important, now, is it? I mean it isn't important to you personally?"

"It's my life. Emotionally, I guess it isn't any more."

Silence, while Nannie stared past Tom. "I killed in rage, Tom. I've never even hit a man, before. Do you think that could be why I—" He broke off, his eyes coming back to search Tom's.

Tom said wearily, "I'm not a priest nor a doctor, Nannie. When did all this start?"

"I thought it was ulcers. I've had stomach trouble for two years. You remember that."

Nannie Koronas, sick and dying. Nannie, the man who loved to live so high on the hog, dying in this big house with nothing but hired help to mourn him.

Nannie's voice was low. "I've been trying to figure it, Tom, a way to take the rap for Lois' death."

Tom started to protest, but Nannie raised a hand. "Or I thought there'd be a way to hang it on Joe Hubbard. But that Garrity girl wouldn't hold still for that. She was with Joe the time Lois died; she still thinks that son-of-a-bitch was something. But, Tom, you can see now, can't you, why I didn't get in touch with you? I was ashamed." His voice was almost a whisper. "And since I've learned what she was, you wouldn't get in touch with me."

Tom rubbed his tender knee. The man in the white jacket carried a tray of food out of the kitchen.

Nannie said, "I've no kids to shame, no wife. I'm dying anyway, for Christ's sake. If I could only set it up, I'd take the rap for both of them. But I was in Frisco the time Lois was in St. Louis. And too damned many people know I was in Frisco. But it might be worth a try, Tom."

Tom thought of the walls and the bleak corridors and the putty faces. He thought of Jean, waiting. He shook his head.

Nannie's fingers were interlaced, his hands limp on the table in front of him.

Tom asked, "Who got Delavan? Do you know?"

Nannie's hands opened, palms spread upward. "I could

134

make a guess. Gilchrist, or that gun of his. Who else? And did you notice where Delavan was dumped? Were you there, Tom?"

Tom nodded.

Nannie blew out his breath wearily. "You pick 'em, don't you? Commie, isn't she?"

"No. Just because she hates gambling syndicates?"

"No, no, no. Hubbard gave me the impression she was kind of punchy."

The white-jacketed man was back and he laid a pair of pills on the table and a glass of water. Nannie picked them up eagerly and swallowed them with the water. He leaned back in his chair.

Tom said, "I'm no better off than I was. Joe Hubbard's death was one they couldn't hang on me, anyway. I wonder how true Connie Garrity's story is?"

"It doesn't matter as long as she sticks to it. With all the other things I've learned about Joe, I wouldn't put anything past him. He even tried to make time with Lisa, one night at a party."

"You and Lisa have broken up, Nannie?"

Nannie shrugged. "She seems to have found new friends, lately. I guess she thought I was going to marry her."

"Ames Gilchrist is one of her friends, Nannie."

"I know. Probably trying to pump her. She thinks she knows a lot about my business and she's no doubt got him convinced she can do him some good there. She's got less than Kefauver got."

Tom smiled. "And she's got it in a safe deposit box. She told me that. And she told me about you and Lois and about you being out of town the time Lois died. And she said you were whining; she was sick of your whining."

"She's riding with the winner—she thinks. Gilchrist ask you to work for him, Tom?"

"He suggested it."

Nannie put a thin hand to his forehead. "Maybe you could learn something from him. There's a good chance he knows some things I don't. Some of the boys have gone over to him already." Nannie chewed his lips. "I'm getting kind of dopey, Tom. That morphine—"

"I'll go, Nannie. I'll see you again." Tom stood up. "I wonder if Jud's through eating?"

"I'll keep him here tonight. I'll get him back in the morning." Nannie's smile was weak. "Jud's one of the *really* loyal ones."

Jud hasn't got a wife, Tom thought. He said nothing, studying the pain-ravished face of the man who had had everything.

Nannie said, "I'm sorry things couldn't have—worked out some other way, Tom. I—Oh, Christ, what's the difference *now?*"

Tom nodded. "I'll see you again, Nannie. Something might break."

"For you, but not for me. Come back and see me, Tom. I don't want to—to step off alone." Shame in Nannie's eyes. And moisture.

"I'll be back," Tom promised. "I'm sorry about everything, Nannie. I guess we both are." He couldn't look at that skull face any more; he turned and walked out of the kitchen.

The white-jacketed man intercepted him in the hall, and opened the door for him. It was dusk, now, and the green of Nannie's immense lawn seemed blade-perfect in the dying light.

Tom walked around to the parking area through the shadow of the house. As he went past the study windows, he could see Jud drinking his coffee and smoking a cigarette. It was quiet in the area, without a sound of traffic coming from the street below.

He took Westwood to Olympic, heading for Venice. Connie worked nights, but perhaps she didn't start this early. It was still light out, but the traffic had thinned to almost nothing in Santa Monica; this was a stay-at-home town.

Venice showed more activity; the bars on Windward Avenue were going at three-quarter throttle. They would be at full speed in another two hours.

In an empty lot next to the apartment, Tom saw the '48 Ford. There were no cars around that looked suspicious; he drove the Plymouth into the same lot.

The blonde was in black, the V of it not quite showing

her navel. Dressed for work. She stood in her kitchen doorway and said, "Welcome home, pilgrim. Miss Revolt throw you out, again?" She stood aside for him to enter.

He moved past the musky fragrance of her perfume into the odor of cooked meat. A partially eaten steak sandwich reposed on a plate on the kitchen table. She closed the door behind him.

"Are you due at work?" Tom asked. "Are you late?"

She shook her head. "Staying the night?"

"No. I—well, I learned some things and——"

"Sit down and have a cup of coffee," she said. She brought the percolator from the stove and poured him a cup.

Tom sat down. "You heard about Delavan, I suppose?"

She looked at him blankly as she picked up her sandwich. She shook her head. "Who's he?"

"A private investigator working for us. He was murdered."

"Working for us? Who's 'us,' Tom?"

"For me."

"*I'll bet,* for you." She took a bite of the sandwich and talked around it. "What do you want from me?"

"I wanted to know if you're sure Joe was in town here when my wife was killed."

She didn't answer immediately. She swallowed the food that was in her mouth and sipped some coffee. Then, "You must be back working for Mr. Koronas, Tom."

"I've seen him. You never told me he questioned you about Joe."

"About men like Koronas, I don't repeat stories. I've known people who did and regretted it. I learned that early, Tom. All I want to do is get along with everybody. If you're here for information, you're wasting your time."

"All I want is the truth about Joe at the time Lois was killed. There's no point in protecting him, now; he's dead."

"I know he's dead. And I know he was here when your wife was killed. That's the gospel truth. Tom, don't come here again with questions, will you? I think I've done my part."

He stood up. "I won't. Thanks for all you've done, Connie."

137

She finished her sandwich and lighted a cigarette. "Don't mention it. Give my love to Miss Revolt." Her voice was dull.

He nodded, and started for the door. He was reaching for the knob, when she said, "Don't we kiss good-by?"

He came back to lift her chin with a forefinger and kiss her on the mouth.

Her voice was softer, now. "God bless you, lamb. And luck."

She didn't look his way as he went out the door. As he moved down the wooden steps, Tom was thinking about the story she'd told him, the champagne story. All she wanted to do was get along with everybody, she claimed. But she nevertheless was playing a dangerous game in that bar.

He believed her about Joe Hubbard. It didn't matter much if he believed her or not; so long as the reverse couldn't be proved, Joe was clear. Joe was safe, anyway, protected by the good earth.

The dying daylight held. He headed for Santa Monica Boulevard, the fast route to Hollywood.

Chapter 12

IN THE lobby of Lisa's apartment, Tom waited, but there was no answer to his ring. He was parked about four hundred feet from the entrance; he went out to wait in the car.

He had an unobstructed view of the doorway from where he sat. He had no way of knowing whether Lisa would be home within a reasonable time. It was only that he had no other place to go for leads. The lead he wanted from her was Ames Gilchrist's address. It wasn't in the phone book.

He waited a half hour and then remembered that Jean knew the man. He drove to a drugstore and phoned her at her friend's house.

Her voice was panicky. "You've been—caught?"

"No. I phoned to find out if you knew Gilchrist's address."

"Tom, the police wanted my car. There's a print of a tire

tread in the mud alongside the driveway and they think it must have been put there in the fog. But they wanted to be sure it wasn't my car. It was a very unusual tread design. I told them a friend had my car, and I think they're looking for it, now. You'd better just leave it, walk away from it."

"That would look fishy as hell, Jean. Maybe I can drive in—"

"No," she interrupted. "Don't drive anywhere. I can get a rental car here in Santa Monica."

He said, "I'm not too far from that apartment of Leonard's. The police won't have discovered that, yet. I still have the key. I'll meet you there."

In front of the apartment on Kenmore, he sat in the car for a while, intending to wait out there. Uneasiness grew in him; he left the car and went into the apartment building.

Their unfinished eggs were still on the kitchen table. He emptied them down the grinder and washed the dishes and the coffee-pot. Then he went out to the front steps to wait for Jean.

She came within a few minutes in a green Ford Tudor. He saw her start to get out on the driver's side, and came quickly down to the car.

"Get in," he said. "Two people talking in a car are less conspicuous."

She slid over, and he sat behind the wheel.

She said, "I phoned a friend for Ames' address." She handed him a slip of paper. "I put it down for you. The police said something about a star imprint on the tire treads; I guess it's very unusual. That isn't what my car has, is it?"

Tom shook his head. "A—star tread? What makes them think it's important?"

"Because it had to happen during the fog, and what other cars came up that driveway during the fog? And remember, even I couldn't stay on it; I went off it once." She lighted a cigarette. "The ground wasn't soft enough before the fog. I haven't watered for days. Where have you been, Tom?"

"I went to see Nannie. He told me——" Tom stopped. "Maybe I'd better not tell you what he told me."

A pause, and then, "About Joe?"

"Yes, it's about Joe, and I'm not going to tell you, now. He also told me that he and Lois were going to be married; he told Joe that."

"But not you."

Tom didn't answer that.

Jean reached over to take his hand. "Did he tell Joe about Lois *before* he sent Joe to St. Louis?"

"Yes."

"I think I know what you're not going to tell me, then."

"Maybe you do, and maybe you don't. Nannie is dying, Jean; he's horribly sick. He said if there was any foolproof way he could take the rap for Lois' death, he'd do it. He'd do that for me."

"And Leonard's?"

"He doesn't know who did that."

"But he knows who killed Joe."

"I didn't say that, Jean. I can't tell you any more without it being a violation of a trust. Jean, Nannie's my friend."

"You're going back to him? Is that what you're telling me?"

"Never, not to gambling, not to anything illegal for any-one. But he was and is my friend. And that's why Joe died."

"That's plain enough. And you're not going to the police with it?" Her grip tightened on his hand. "Don't you see it? You're still morally on Nannie's side of the fence."

"No, I'm not. Are you on Joe's side? I'm concerned with clearing myself. Right now, I'm on *my* side of the fence and mine alone. I'm not betraying any friends, especially those who could be allies. That's simple self-interest and that's what's going to motivate me until I'm clear. If I'm ever clear."

Silence for seconds and then a choked sound from her and headlights went by and he saw her tears. He leaned over to kiss her wet cheek.

She whispered, "Working with people like that—no good can come of it, Tom."

"Maybe not. But it's the only way I have." He handed her the keys to the Plymouth. "I'll phone you later. I suppose I could sleep in this apartment tonight?"

"Or my place." She gave him a key. "I have another hidden in the garage. Be careful, Tom, won't you?"

140

"You can bet on that." He kissed her, and watched her get out and walk to the Plymouth. He didn't start the Ford until the Plymouth's tail lights had disappeared around the corner.

The address she'd given him was in west Los Angeles, in the Cheviot Hills district. It was an expensive district of large homes and winding, hilly streets, of well-kept palm trees and perfect lawns.

The address Jean had given him was one of the few new homes in the district, a low place of fire-engine-red barn siding with a shake roof, the eaves of which extended to the top of the shrubbery in front of the house. Ames Gilchrist was getting acclimated in a hurry.

There was a car in the driveway and Tom pulled up behind it. It was a Buick Roadmaster convertible with white sidewall air wheels, and the stars of the tread were visible in the glare of the Ford's headlights.

Tom killed the motor and saw the light go on in the shrubbery-shrouded areaway around the front door. He was walking across the stepping stones that led from the driveway when the front door opened.

Ames Gilchrist stood in the open doorway, squinting out at the dark lawn. As Tom came into the light spilling out from the areaway, Ames said, "Well, this is a surprise. I was expecting someone else."

"Lisa?"

Ames didn't answer that. He looked at Tom thoughtfully. "Here to do business, Tom?"

"Maybe. I can't work for you until I'm clear, though. I'd be no good to you the way I am."

"I know. Come in."

Tom went in to a long, beamed living room, furnished in Early American. Ames indicated a chair, and asked, "Drink?"

Tom sat down, his hand not far from the .38 in his waistband. "No, thanks. How do you figure I could work for you?"

Ames sat on the figured davenport and reached forward to take a cigarette from a box on the maple coffee table. He studied it like a ham actor before putting it between his lips.

He lighted it, inhaled, and said, "I guess we can pin your
141

wife's death to Nannie without too much trouble."

"You underestimate Nannie."

"Maybe. I was told by one of the boys when I first came out, that all of Nannie's boys are loyal, too. You'd be surprised to learn how many are working for me right now."

Tom smiled. "You really moved in, didn't you? Even with Lisa."

Something close to a frown on the thin face. "Lisa—never liked anything but Nannie's money. She and I understand each other."

Tom said, "I learned that Nannie was in Frisco at the time my wife was killed. He'll have witnesses up there."

"Maybe. Some of his Frisco boys are working for me, too, now. Nannie's a has-been, Tom. They don't get much loyalty."

Tom thought of Jud and said nothing.

Gilchrist said softly, "I even hear that Nannie's seriously sick. Is that true, do you know?"

Tom shrugged. "I doubt it. I heard he had some stomach trouble, but he's had it before. He eats too well." Tom glanced at the open evening paper on the davenport beside Gilchrist. "Anything new on Delavan?"

Gilchrist glanced at the paper and back at Tom. "That was the first I'd heard of it."

"Is that your car out there?" Tom asked.

The thin man studied him. "The Buick? Yes. Why?"

"That's the kind of car the body was brought to the house in."

Ames Gilchrist's face was totally blank. "How do you know?"

"I was there."

"This town is filled with Buicks," Gilchrist said. "There's nothing in the paper about a Buick."

"I didn't tell the police it was a Buick. I didn't see them, naturally. And I didn't tell Jean I saw the car."

Ames smiled. "But you saw it? *Really*, now?"

Tom nodded, his right hand in his lap, near the gun.

After a moment, Gilchrist said, "I don't think I'm following you, Tom. I think we can be frank with each other."

"I'm being frank. It's your turn."

"Fair enough." Ames leaned forward to put out the cigarette in an ash tray. "First of all you suggest you don't know if Nannie is sick or not. I happen to know you were at his house today. You tell me you saw a Buick at Jean's house; the fog in that canyon was too thick for you to see five feet away from you."

"How do you know it was? Were you there?"

"I may have been, though not with a body. At any rate, you were there and you know it was that foggy. You sound as though you're trying to trap me. I thought you were looking for work." Ames leaned back against the cushions. "I think you're still working for Nannie Koronas."

"So far," Tom answered, "I'm just working for me. Your man comes up to Jean's house, posing as a cop; you go around trying doorknobs and then a body is dumped. What do you want me to do, recommend you for my lodge?"

Ames smiled. "All I want you to do is decide who you're going to work for. You wouldn't be coming in as a partner, you know, but as an employee."

"If I'm cleared," Tom said, "you'd welcome me as a partner. Because I'd be a millionaire."

Ames frowned and his eyes narrowed. "That's right— your wife was rich, wasn't she? And you'd—" He paused.

"She hasn't any relatives," Tom said.

Ames nodded slowly, his eyes thoughtful. "I see—Well, that would put a different angle on things, probably." He smiled. "Did you want to buy into the firm, Tom?"

"First, I want to know how you're going to clear me. Nannie would be too slippery to be sure of."

He shrugged. "There are other stooges. I need an entry into the big money betters, Tom."

"Other stooges, you said. Maybe you've got one in mind?"

"I might. Tom, we're getting nowhere. Are you in, or out? If you're in, say so, and let me worry about the rest of it. You can stay here. You'll be safe here. I'll set up the patsy for you."

Tom smiled. "It might even be the real killer."

Ames Gilchrist's face stiffened. "We're going around again, Tom. Do you know who the real killer is?"

"I think it's the same one who killed Delavan."

"And who's that?"

Tom shook his head. "I don't know. I'm not sure."

"Did you come here to find out?"

Tom nodded.

Gilchrist's head was back against the cushion of the davenport and he closed his eyes. "I don't think we can do business, Tom. You didn't come here to do business. Good-by. Stay out of trouble." He opened his eyes. "If you can."

Tom stood up. "It bothered you to learn I was rich, didn't it? It put a new angle on it."

Something flickered in Gilchrist's eyes, but his face remained impassive. "Good-by, Tom. Get out."

Tom kept his hand under the jacket, on the butt of the .38 as he went out.

The street was quiet and deserted as he climbed into the Ford and backed it out of the driveway. Good solid neighborhood of solvent taxpayers and committee-sought citizens, older homes and older trees, winding, peaceful streets. And a tarantula in the middle in a blood-red new house.

Olympic to Westwood and Westwood toward Nannie's. All men had their Achilles' heel; the vanity of Ames Gilchrist could be his. But what could be proved? What did he have the law could work on? Nothing.

Headlights came up from behind, swung by; he kept the Ford at an even thirty-five miles an hour and stuck to the right hand lane.

On Wilshire, he was stopped by the light. A preponderance of new cars in the solid flow of traffic on Wilshire and a heavy sprinkling of cars in the luxury class. Traffic alone was almost enough of a problem for the ten thousand men in the Department; how much time was left for murder?

And this hadn't been their murder, this first one. It hadn't happened in the city on wheels. Extradition would be granted quickly; this Department had enough troubles of its own.

He should check the airport, and he couldn't. Because he couldn't identify himself. The light changed and he moved across Wilshire into the college town of Westwood.

Climbing and then the flat house to his right, and he turned in on the green macadam drive. The glass brick of the walls winked back at him as his headlights moved across them. There was a light on in the study where Jud had eaten.

144

Nannie sat there in a big chair, staring into a small coal fire in the fireplace.

The white-jacketed deaf man opened the door and said, "Mr. Koronas is in the den. He said if you came, you should go right in."

Nannie glanced up as Tom entered the study. His eyes looked peaceful and drugged. "Staying here tonight, Tom?"

"If I may. I've been over to see Gilchrist."

Nannie said nothing, his gaze on the fire.

Tom asked, "May I use this phone?"

"Of course. I'm glad you're staying, tonight, Tom. I hate to be alone, without friends."

Tom dialed the number of Jean's friend. When he had her on the phone, he said, "Phone the police right now. Tell them Ames Gilchrist has a Buick with special tires, tires with a star tread."

"Great, Tom. Oh, fine. Where are you now?"

"At Nannie's. I'm staying here tonight."

"Oh." A long pause. "Tom, why?"

"Because he's my friend, and I think he'd like the company. I've mistreated him long enough."

"All right. You—love me?"

"I love you. Take care of yourself."

"And you, too. Be *so* careful."

"Yes. Good night, darling."

When he replaced the phone in its cradle, he looked over to see that Nannie's eyes were closed.

Tom came around to sit in a chair nearby. He lighted a cigarette and stared at the fire.

Nannie said, "Tom Spears, running to the law. Now, I've heard it."

"It's murder, Nannie. My wife."

"Yes. Of course, that makes it different, I suppose. You love this Jean, eh?"

"I do."

"Hubbard's girl friend. They were engaged, weren't they?"

"Yup." Tom inhaled the smoke slowly, deeply.

"I should have married," Nannie said. "But who'd buy a cow, the milk I had? I should have married and had some kids. Oh Christ, why didn't I ever have any kids?"

Tom stared at the fire.

Nannie asked, "Learn anything except what kind of tires Gilchrist's Buick has?"

"Nothing definite. Would Neilson do some work for me, tomorrow? How much influence have you still got around town, Nannie?"

"Neilson will do anything I tell him to do. I still have friends in some spots in town. What do you want?"

"Airline reservations for the time my wife was killed. I want to see who was out of town. The only way the killer could have got there in time was to take a plane. Damn it, it would need to be the same plane, almost. I took the next one."

"They've been checked," Nannie said sleepily. "I wanted to know who killed her, too, Tom. There were some names that looked suspicious, one that turned out to be a complete phony, even the confirming telephone number was phony. But where can you go from there?"

"Were the seat listings given?"

"I got 'em through the stewardess. The phony name sat up front, Lois in the rear of the plane. Lois was going back to St. Louis to put the house up for sale. One of her sudden whims, I learned later. She was going to put it into jewels and furs, to cheat you out of any community property rights."

"Would that do it?"

"I don't know. She thought so."

"Who told you this, Nannie?"

Nannie started to answer, and then his head swiveled and he stared at Tom. "You don't think—? It couldn't have been—?"

"What was the phony name?"

"K.T. Arnold."

"And the name in the flanking seat?"

"I don't remember. I still have the list, but what difference would—Oh Lord, how stupid can I be? You know, Tom, I never even thought of that."

"Maybe," Tom said slowly, "none of it will come to anything. The town is full of phony names."

Nannie leaned back again, and his voice was quieter. "I'll have Luke get the list, as soon as he comes in. It's worth a try, Tom. What else did Gilchrist tell you?"

"He knew I was here to see you. Do you trust your help?"

"I do. He must have had a man watching outside. Or maybe a man following you. Damn it, I can't stay awake, and I've got to."

"No, you don't, Nannie. Tomorrow will do as well. I'm going to bed."

Nannie's voice was just a whisper. "Tomorrow——? How many tomorrows are there?"

Chapter 13

IN THE big bedroom in the north wing of the big house, Tom lay in the dark, hoping tomorrow would be the brightest he'd had in months. Every man outside the walls had some bright tomorrows to keep him going, the workless week ends, payday, vacations. Inside the walls there was the single tomorrow that meant freedom; all the tomorrows after that one had to be better.

With Nannie, every tomorrow was lagniappe. Though none of them but the last one would bring him any peace.

Tomorrow could be another dead end for Tom, too. He'd learned some things and they had helped to form a picture but the truth of the picture was unproved.

The sight of Nannie lingered in his mind, the sick and wasted image of what had been a big and confident man. Jean had been wrong about Nannie; the measure of the man was his concern for his friends at a time when most men are completely self-concerned.

In the hall, outside, he heard quiet footsteps and a little later, the sound of running water. Somewhere, a door closed. From outside came the sound of young voices, singing, and the clatter of an antiquated car. Students, with no thoughts of tomorrow. The voices grew dimmer and Tom slept.

Nannie showed no outward signs of pain at breakfast. His eyes were dull; Tom guessed he was drugged. Neilson ate with them and Nannie had the seating list.

The passenger in the flanking seat was named Albert

Buechner and he had given a hotel as a local address. His home address was St. Louis.

"That looks like a blind alley," Nannie said.

Neilson was frowning thoughtfully. "I smell something, boss. That name has an odor. Let me check it this morning."

Nannie's dull eyes showed no interest. "What do you smell?"

"A rat, I think. A rat named Al. Remember Al, boss? He wanted to make a deal?"

Nannie nodded. "I remember. A Gilchrist stooge."

"That's right. And nosy, too. I've met him a couple places when I was looking for Golden Boy, here." Neilson's thumb indicated Tom contemptuously.

Tom kept his voice even. "He might be the one who came to see Jean. He posed as a cop and scared me out of the house. Or was that one of yours, Nannie?"

Nannie shook his head, looking from Tom to Neilson and back. Then he said, "I wonder if Jean would go along with— No, I suppose we couldn't even ask her that."

"I'll ask her," Tom said, and stood up. "I'll phone her right now." He went to the study, out of their hearing range.

She sounded sleepy. She said, "Trouble?"

Tom took a breath. "No. A favor, Jean. I want you to go along with one of Nannie's men and identify somebody."

"Tom, for heaven's sake, you can't expect me to work with—"

"No, I can't. I'm asking you to, though. It could be the man who posed as a policeman."

Silence for seconds, and then her quiet voice. "Do you want me to come there?"

"No. I'll have him pick you up. I want to get this Ford out of here, anyway. He can drive that. Gilchrist might have given the police the number, though I'm almost sure he didn't see it. But it's no time to take chances."

"Tom, you sound—hopeful."

"It's a very small hope, but it's the first, honey. Neilson will pick you up."

A silence, again. And then, "All right. God, I hope you know what you're doing." She gave him the address.

In the kitchen, Nannie's eyes were on Tom from the moment he entered. Tom nodded, and looked at Neilson. "You'd better take that Ford I was wheeling." He told him Jean's address.

Neilson looked at Nannie. "That's Hubbard's girl friend, you know, boss."

Nannie nodded. "Nobody knows it better than I do, Luke. Pick her up."

"Okay." Neilson rose. "I'd better get to work. Nannie, don't worry, will you? It's no good, worrying."

A shadow of a smile came to the emaciated face. "I'll try not to worry, Luke. Thank you."

Neilson took the keys from Tom without looking at him, and went out.

Nannie said, "Do you believe in God, Tom?"

"I don't know. I try to." Tom sat down and sipped his coffee. "It helps, if you can."

"Oh, sure. And a slug through the brain would help, too. I could do it to Hubbard. Why can't I do it to me? What the hell is keeping me going?"

"I guess what keeps us all going, Nannie. Hope."

"Hope. Christ."

Tom said quietly, "Maybe you're thinking of us, Nannie. And if there is a God, that won't hurt you any with Him."

"If there is a God," Nannie answered, "He isn't likely to forget I murdered a man. Maybe it's better for me if there isn't a God. I'd rather rot than burn."

Tom lighted a cigarette and tried to keep his gaze away from Nannie.

The ghost of a smile, again, and Nannie said, "Well, I suppose I should figure it happens to all of us. But damn it, this is happening to *me*." He put a hand on the table and rose. "Let's go into the den. I've got some Satchmo you'd like."

In the study, they sat with a pot of coffee, listening to the magic horn and gravel voice of America's most beloved musician. And then some Pee Wee Hunt corn and Ellington with some blues. Nannie sat there quietly, soaking in it; Nannie want no dirges.

They were still sitting there when Neilson and Jean came.

149

Jean stood in the doorway to the study a moment before following Neilson into the room. Then she moved swiftly to Tom's side.

Tom rose. "Well?"

She nodded. "The same man. What does it mean, Tom?"

"It means he was lucky. He was on the right plane. Jean, I want you to meet my best friend. This is Nannie Koronas."

Jean nodded, hesitated, and then moved forward to accept Nannie's proffered handshake.

Neilson said, "I think I can place the guy, now, Nannie. Used to work for Jethroe in Chi, and when Jethroe got run out, he went to St. Louis. That's Gilchrist's stamping grounds, you know."

Nannie nodded. "I know." He looked at Tom. "But I still don't get it."

Tom said, "He isn't the first to come out, Nannie. How many scouts have come out from the East, checking the local situation with an eye to moving in? We remember quite a few of them, don't we, Nannie?"

Nannie's dull eyes were thoughtful. "I do."

"So," Tom went on, "he hung around a while and got to know who the boys were and who they were sleeping with. But the big thing he learned was how loyal the boys were to you, Nannie. That was the report he was probably going to take back. And then he had a stroke of luck."

A flicker in the dull eyes. "He took the right plane and happened to get the right seat. And when the stewardess came along, checking the passenger reservations, he heard his seat-mate confirm the phony name."

Tom nodded. "And that was the wedge."

Neilson said, "You gentlemen aren't making sense to me."

"I hope we're making sense to us," Nannie said. "Luke, this Al Buechner, he plays it heavy? What's his reputation?"

"I'm not sure, boss. It's a long time since I heard his name. Anybody can be cracked, I guess, if he's hit right."

Jean's face stiffened, and Nannie didn't miss it. He said gently, "It's Tom's neck, Jean."

"Yes, and there's a police department in this town. They've already picked up Ames Gilchrist."

Tom smiled. "Well, that helps. That's a weapon. If we can

get the others up here before Gilchrist talks himself out of the can, we might have an edge."

Neilson said, "You'd have some chance of getting Buechner up here without using a gun."

Nannie looked at Tom. "But I think K. T. Arnold will come, if I explain it's about my will. That should do it."

Jean said quietly, "Are Mr. Neilson and I outsiders? I'm sure he's as much in the dark as I am about your conversation."

"We'll explain it all at lunch," Nannie said. "The sun's out, and we'll have lunch on the patio. Four good friends, constructing a rat trap."

Chapter 14

JEAN'S COOL reserve held through lunch, while Luke and Nannie and Tom considered all the angles. They'd need Buechner, they decided, but what could they induce him with?

"The organization," Tom suggested. "You know Jethroe, don't you, Nannie? Isn't he out in the Valley, breeding chinchillas, or something? Retired, isn't he?"

Nannie nodded. "Retired and breeding chinchillas. I know him quite well."

"Enough to ask him for a favor?"

"I'm sure of it."

"So he'd give Buechner the word on you, that you can be trusted and you tell Buechner that you're looking for a live wire to take over the organization."

"That stinks," Neilson said. "The guy can't be that dumb."

"If I promise him the organization," Nannie said, "I'll deliver it. His boss in the clink; he's going to listen, isn't he?"

Neilson said, "You'd give Buechner what's left of the organization just to get Spears off the hook, to help a man who wouldn't even come near you until yesterday?"

"To help my friend," Nannie said. "You don't know the whole story, Luke."

"I'll say I don't," Neilson said. "But it's your outfit, Nannie, and I guess that's enough for me."

Tom looked at Jean and saw that some of the chill had left her eyes. He smiled at her. Her answering smile was weak.

Nannie rose slowly and stood for a moment, looking down at Jean. "You're doing better, this time," he said quietly. "If you have any boys, I suppose it would be horrible to name one Nannie? Put the punk behind the eight ball, right from the start."

She managed a smile. "I'll give it some thought. *We'll* give it some thought." She looked at Tom and down at the tablecloth.

Tom said, "Is that just a nickname, Nannie?"

"For Amos. Nannie's better. I've got to make some phone calls." He went into the house.

"Great guy," Neilson said. "Nobody asked me, though. Who wants a drink? I do." He rose. "I'll get the stuff."

Jean looked at Tom and away. She picked at the tablecloth absent-mindedly. Tom offered no conversation.

Finally, Jean looked up again. "I suppose I could be wrong."

"You were wrong enough on Joe Hubbard. Where was your Carrie Nation complex then?"

"He was an easy man to be wrong about. He had you fooled. You're so damned bright."

"Lately. Does that bother you? Don't you want a *man* around the house?"

"I wanted a lamb, I guess. Shut up. *Joe* was a *man*."

"You shut up. About him, anyway. Honey, I'll be any damned thing you want me to be except certain. I don't intend to be certain about anything."

Neilson came out from the house, wheeling a portable bar. Tom went over to help him get it across the rough flagstones.

Jean said, "Make mine whiskey, bourbon, double."

Tom winked at her and reached for a bottle.

In the study, Nannie said, "Just Luke and I will be out in the open. You kids want to listen in, there's a small closet next to the fireplace." He looked at Jean. "Though maybe you shouldn't. This K. T. Arnold sometimes uses some strong language."

Jean smiled. "I can take it. Haven't you overlooked one big factor? Whatever they admit here isn't important if you can't take it into court."

"Not even a wire recording of it?"

"I don't think it would be admissible evidence. They can be doctored too easily. Any smart attorney knows that."

Nannie said thoughtfully, "Then we'll have only the ambition of this Al Buechner. That's the man I'll have to sell."

"And immunity, too, you'll have to sell him. It would take some talking. How can he be sure you won't doublecross him?"

"I've never crossed anybody in my life. And I wouldn't be surprised if Jethroe told him that. You see, Jean, Jethroe's one of the old-fashioned kind, too, an honest gambler. That's why he was run out of Chicago; he didn't have a gun in the organization."

Tom said, "Jean, I think we can leave this safely in Nannie's hands. Shall we inspect the closet?"

There was the sound of a door chime, and Nannie said, "This might be the right time for that."

It was a ventilated closet and one of the air inlets was over the door to the study. "Perfect for eavesdroppers," Tom said, and pulled her close.

Her lips clung, her slight body trembled. "Oh, Tom, what kind of way is this to work?"

"My way. Nannie's way. I'll sell you on him, yet."

"I'm half sold. I—"

From the other side of the door, Nannie said, "Quiet. They're coming in, now."

The pressure of the gun against Tom's waist had irritated the skin. He took the gun out and put it in his trouser pocket.

Jean whispered, "You won't need that, Tom. Give it to me."

He shook his head.

Then, from the study, he heard Nannie say, "Well, Mr. Buechner, we meet face to face for a change. I hope it will be to your advantage. And Lisa. Why so unhappy, Lisa? You can see I'm dying. And think of all that lovely money I'll be leaving behind. Four million, Lisa. For just a little information you should have."

Lisa said, "I thought there was an angle. I told you, didn't I, Al? You don't know this bastard."

A voice Tom didn't recognize that must belong to Al Buechner. "Take it easy, Lisa. Let's hear the man out. Fred Jethroe has never steered me wrong yet."

"You can listen to him, then," Lisa said. "I'm going."

Nannie's quiet, courteous voice: "If you prefer, Lisa. You should listen, because we'll be talking about you. For your own protection you should listen—but of course, if—"

"I'll stay," Lisa said after a few seconds. "Try to keep the ham out of it, though, eh?"

"I'll try, Lisa. Won't you both sit down?"

Silence, the scrape of a chair and then Lisa said, "What's the muscle doing here? Do we need him?"

"I'd prefer to have him here," Nannie said. "Is it all right with you, Mr. Buechner?"

"He doesn't bother me," Buechner said. "I've seen enough of him."

Luke Neilson laughed, and there was a moment's silence.

Then Lisa said, "All right, let's get on with it."

Nannie's voice was low but clear. "Fair enough. We'll start with you, Lisa, and go back to a time when I was in Frisco and you got a call from Lois Spears." A pause. "Do you remember the day?"

"I might. Keep talking."

"Lois didn't know I had you set up. She probably figured the girl who answered the phone was a maid, or something. Anyway, she left the message about going to St. Louis, and why. You told me that, yourself. Stupid of you."

"There wasn't any reason to keep it a secret." A faint tremor in Lisa's voice.

"Wasn't there? Why, then, did you take the same plane and use the name K. T. Arnold? I think I can tell you why. Because to a stewardess, and especially on this run, it doesn't seem unusual for a girl to use only initials. And if some-body else should check it, later, they'd naturally figure it for a man. Like I did, at first."

Buechner: "Don't look at me, Lisa."

Lisa's voice was harsh. "You damned fool; why do you

154

think he wanted us *both* here at the same time?"

Nannie said, "I told you you could leave. The offer is still open, Lisa."

Silence.

Nannie went on quietly. "You thought I was going to marry you until you heard about Lois. And it must have burned you to think a girl as rich as she was was going to get the money you had designs on. So you took the plane, knowing I'd be out of town for a week."

A pause, and then someone said, "It's time for your pills, boss." It was the white-jacketed man. Silence and then the sound of water from a carafe pouring into a glass. Jean's hand came over to find Tom's.

Nannie's voice: "This was a break for you, Al, because that was the plane you were on. And you knew her right name and heard her give the phony one. And you knew Tom Spears' wife was on the plane. And you were bright enough to add one and one. The thing is, Al, did you follow her all the way to Lois' house in St. Louis?"

Nothing. Silence. Jean squeezed Tom's hand tightly.

Then Al's careful voice. "Jethroe didn't tell you I was any kind of a pigeon, did he, Mr. Koronas?"

"No, he didn't. As a matter of fact, I don't know too much about you, Al. Working for Jethroe would be on your side; working for Ames Gilchrist definitely isn't."

Silence. Jean moved closer to Tom.

Nannie, then: "A thing I hesitated to bring up, Al—you undoubtedly know that impersonating a police officer can be a very serious offense."

Buechner said, "Heat, huh? You don't miss much, do you, Mr. Koronas?"

"I try not to miss anything. I hate to call copper, but I'm not sure Miss Revolt shares my feelings about the law. I can promise to keep her off your neck, I think, though."

"Mmmm-hmmm. What else can you promise, Mr. Koronas?"

"I was going to promise you the organization, but I've been thinking about that. It doesn't seem fair to some of the old, loyal members. How does a hundred thousand dollars in cash,

155

in non-taxable cash sound to you?"

"It listens real good, Mr. Koronas. Of course, nobody can spend talk, huh?"

Some hysteria in Lisa's voice. "Al, for God's sake, don't you see what the man's doing? Ames will be free in a few hours, and I don't have to tell you how *he* feels about me, Al. You wouldn't live to spend the money."

"That's a point. He feels about you a lot. Lot of boys do. Sister, face a fact; Ames is getting awful fed up with your catting around."

Luke Neilson, then: "Al, did you drive Ames' Buick over to the Revolt girl's place? Did you borrow it that afternoon?"

"Hell, no. What gave you that idea?"

Luke's calm voice: "A cop out of the West Side Station. You might lay low for a couple of days, Al."

Lisa: "They're lying, Al. Damn it, don't you see——"

Luke: "If you want, I'll phone him for you, Al. I know him pretty well."

Al said quietly, "Don't bother. A hundred grand. You couldn't raise the ante, huh?"

"I could. And the way it will be, it's money you lent me over the years and I finally made it up to you, if you want to declare it. I'll swear to that. How much raise, Al?"

"Hundred and a half. Because I'll want to be a long way away from here and it's tough getting a job in a country where you don't know the language, right?"

Nannie chuckled. "Right. Did you follow Lisa all the way to Lois' house, Al?"

"Well, now, I haven't seen any money, Mr. Koronas, and a man has to be careful, these days. Not that your reputation isn't sound enough, understand, but——"

Nannie said, "I'll have the money brought in. I'll wait until you can get a messenger to take it wherever you want it taken. And then we'll phone the police together. Isn't that safe all around?"

"That's real efficient," Al said. "That's big time operating. Well, Mr. Koronas, I did follow her to the house. And when——"

Lisa said, "Shut up, Al."

A long silence and then Nannie's voice. "Lisa, that gun is
156

pointing at me. What can I lose? You'd be doing me a favor. Are you trying to scare me with a gun?"

Lisa said, "Don't move, Luke. Or you, Al. Don't move a muscle."

Luke's voice: "A .32, isn't it? Is that the one that got Delavan, Al?"

"Who knows?" Al said. "That one I can't swear to, though I guess we're all sure enough about it. Ames probably dumped the body and got panicky and named me to the cops. I never trusted him, nor her, either. But a man has to eat. Lordy, how I could eat on a hundred and fifty grand."

"Stop talking, Al. Shut up."

A moment's silence and then Lisa's voice again. "All right, Nannie, stand up. You big son-of-a-bitch, I want to see you topple. Stand up, or I'll shoot you in the chair."

There was the scrape of a chair and Luke's shouted "No, Nannie, no!" And there was the sound of two shots filling the room.

Tom came out, the .38 ready, but Luke's fist was faster. Luke swung his big body in a complete arc and brought one ham-like fist whistling around with the swing of his body. It caught Lisa Prentice flush on the mouth, and she went back over the chair behind her and through the full-length window. Luke went through the window after her.

On the floor near his overturned chair, Nannie moaned, and blood flecked his lips. Tom knelt beside him, and Nannie said, "One kid for me, huh, Tom? One Nannie, to go on living?"

"I promise."

Nannie smiled, and blood ran down from a corner of his mouth. "In the lungs, I think." He shook his head. "The nicest thing the little bitch ever did for me. I wish——"

Tom never learned the last wish. Nannie's eyes closed and a horrible shudder shook his wasted body and when the eyes opened again they were staring into eternity. . . .

In the canyon house, Jean and Tom sat in the kitchen. The table had been moved over to the window again, and there was a fifth, well gone, between them.

"Slobs," Jean said. "Nannie dead and we run out before

the law comes and now we sit and drink."

"You don't have to, Jean. I have to, but you don't have to."

"I guess I do, Tom. How wrong I was about him. What made you think of Lisa as the killer?"

"Her greed and learning that Nannie meant to marry Lois. Lisa thought that it was just a question of time with Nannie and she'd be really set up. And the way she lied about Nannie's being out of town. I mean, she *knew* he was in Frisco, but she wanted me to get a different idea. And why was Ames worried about me if he wasn't trying to protect somebody else? And who would that be? Lisa, because he needed her to get the inside story of Nannie's operations."

"Tom, were you and Lisa—?" She stopped. "I mean, did you—"

He said quickly, "Here comes Neilson. We'll get some story, now."

The Gray Chev pulled into the parking area and stopped as Tom went to the front door. Neilson's bland face looked grim as he came along the walk.

Tom asked him, "Did Lisa crack yet?"

"Wide open." Neilson took a deep breath. "She's nailed for Nannie's death, anyway, so she may as well open up. I guess it was just as well Nannie went the way he did, eh?"

Tom held the door wide for Luke to enter. "That's right. How about Al?"

"He's talking like a gentleman. And taking care of Gilchrist at the same time." They were in the kitchen, now, and Neilson's gaze went to the bottle on the table.

Jean said, "Neat?" and reached for a glass.

"Neat," he said. He slumped into the chair at the end of the table.

Jean poured him a double shot. "Lisa killed Delavan, then? He must have learned about her trip to St. Louis and gone up to question her?"

Neilson nodded, and gulped the whiskey. "That's right. And she got scared and shot him. And Ames was sucker enough about Lisa to want to dump the body for her. Well, there's only one safe spot to do that—Topanga Canyon. And there's only *one* way to get to Topanga from Los Angeles. He had to go past here. Then he hit the fog when he came into Santa Monica. Coming down from the bluff it was worse and he figured he might not make Topanga. And even if he did, the Coast road would be lousy with cops handling the jammed traffic, so he dumped Delavan here. Which made it look like a warning, and also loused up the case for the law."

Jean poured another drink into the empty glass. "And Tom? Don't you think Tom should give himself up, now?"

Neilson shook his head. "Not tonight. I'll get a lawyer, first, a *good* lawyer this time, a guy smart enough to know how to deal." He paused. "A guy like Nannie."

Jean grinned wryly. "Okay, Luke. I know when I'm told off."

Neilson said nothing, staring at his glass.

Jean said softly, "Why don't we drink to Nannie? Why don't we get good and stinking drunk?"

Printed in the United States
By Bookmasters